TARGET

Just then, the two firemen came out of the front door, carrying a body between them. It was a young man in blackened pyjamas. Paramedics moved in swiftly to take over. They examined the victim carefully before fitting an oxygen mask on his face. The young man was lifted on to a stretcher and the police moved the crowd back so he could be carried to the ambulance.

TARGET

KEITH MILES

HarperCollins*Publishers*

First published in Great Britain 1995 by
HarperCollins*Publishers* Ltd
77-85 Fulham Palace Road, Hammersmith,
London W6 8JB

Copyright © Keith Miles 1995

The author asserts the moral right to be identified
as the author of this work.

ISBN 0 00 675159 8

Set in Stempel Garamond
Printed and bound in Great Britain by
HarperCollins Manufacturing, Glasgow

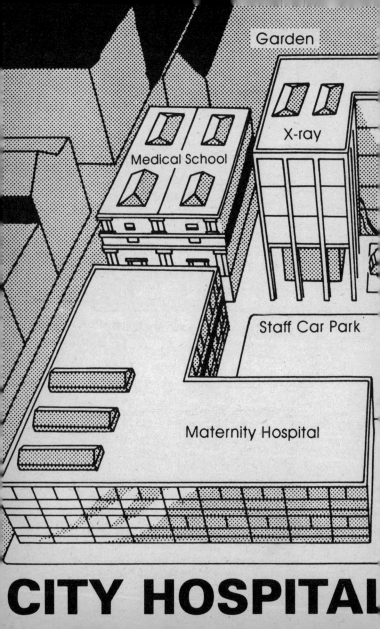

Garden

X-ray

Medical School

Staff Car Park

Maternity Hospital

CITY HOSPITAL

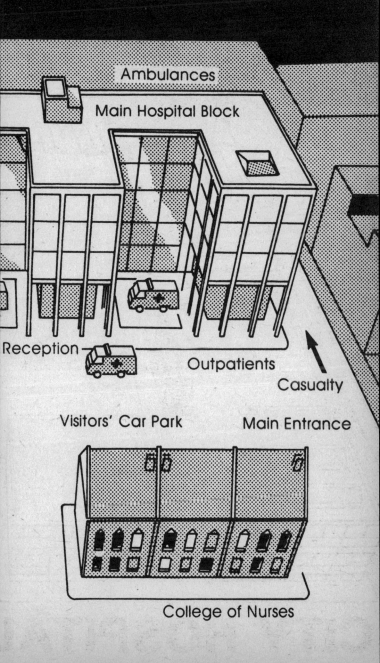

CHAPTER ONE

The sudden bang took them by surprise. It was so loud and so close that Gordy Robbins thought one of his tyres had blown out. He jammed his foot on the brake and brought the car to a juddering halt. Suzie Hembrow got out of the vehicle with him.

'What's the problem?' she asked.

'I'm not sure.' He kicked all four tyres in succession and found them hard. 'I thought I'd a blow-out.'

'Maybe the silencer went.'

'No chance, Suzie. I only had it replaced a month ago.'

'What could have caused that terrible noise?'

'Yes, what on earth could it have been?'

Gordy got an immediate answer. Sounds of commotion reached them from a nearby street. A scream rose above the general hubbub. Gordy reacted quickly.

'Suzie, get back in the car!' he said.

She pointed. 'It seemed to come from Gallagher Road.'

'OK, let's go and see.'

Suzie jumped back into the passenger seat and shut the door. Gordy started the engine again and drove down the first side street. As soon as he turned into Gallagher Road, they saw what had happened. Halfway down the road, a house was on fire. It was a dark night but the flames lit everything up with a hideous glare.

People were pouring out of all the neighbouring houses. Some were in their pyjamas and dressing gowns. Gordy parked his car by the kerb and they both leaped out and raced across to the house. It was gruesome.

'Look at that window!' gasped Suzie.

'What window?' he said. 'It's been blown to pieces.'

'There must have been some sort of explosion.'

'It's smashed *everything*!'

Suzie pointed at the adjoining properties. All had lost their windows in the blast and even the houses opposite were surrounded by shattered glass. Cars parked nearby had smashed windscreens, but the burning house had sustained serious damage. Its bay window had been completely destroyed.

Everyone seemed to be in a state of shock; confusion and fear had seized them. Children were crying and a young woman was still screaming at the top of her voice – her boyfriend tried in vain to console her. The couple had been sitting in their stationary car when all its windows had cracked with the force of the blast.

Gordy and Suzie pushed their way through the crowd. A stocky man was looking warily at the burning house, wondering if it was safe to dart inside.

'Is anyone in there?' asked Gordy.

'I think so,' said the man.

'What happened?'

'God knows!'

'It sounded like a clap of thunder,' said Suzie.

'Gas explosion, I think,' decided the man.

He launched himself at the front door, which was hanging on its hinges. Pulling it fully open, he tried to dash inside but he was beaten back by thick smoke. Gordy rushed forward to help him back to safety.

'It's too dangerous!' he said.

'We can't just abandon him!'

'You've got no choice.'

Suzie was the first to hear the police siren. It was quickly followed by the distinctive wail of a fire engine.

'Leave it to the professionals,' she said.

The man took another step towards the house but his wife came out of the crowd and grabbed him by the arm. She looked anxious as she stood there in her quilted dressing gown.

'Get back, Colin!' she pleaded.

'There must be *some* way to help him, love.'

'You'll get yourself killed!'

'But he's our neighbour.'

'We hardly know him,' she argued. 'Now come on back.'

She tugged him away from the house. The police car cut a path through the crowd and pulled up just beyond the burning property. Four uniformed officers emerged to take control. Their first job was to clear people away so that the fire engine could get through.

Gordy and Suzie were ushered across to the other pavement. They watched in admiration as the firemen went into action. Within a minute of arriving at the scene, they assessed the situation and trained their hoses on the seat of the blaze.

An ambulance siren now added to the cacophony. It picked its way along the street and drew up behind the police car. The rear doors were opened in readiness.

Suzie viewed it all with growing horror.

'What a dreadful way to die!' she exclaimed.

'We don't even know if anyone's in there,' said Gordy.

'That neighbour thought that there was.'

'Let's hope he was wrong.

'Yes – nobody could survive that.'

It was a neat, modern, detached house in a fashionable area. The garage beside it had also been devastated by the blast. It had virtually collapsed on to the new Mercedes. The whole of the front garden was littered with fragments of wood and glass.

The emergency services had responded promptly and the firemen had got there before the blaze could really take a hold and they brought it swiftly under control. As flames gave way to hissing smoke, two of the crew put on breathing apparatus and went into the house. They carried axes to hack their way through any obstruction.

Suzie turned away involuntarily.

'I can't bear to watch any more,' she said.

'It'll soon be over,' assured Gordy, slipping an arm round her shoulders. 'Do you want to go back to the car?'

'Not yet. Not until...we know the worst.'

He sighed. 'I'm afraid we already do.'

But Gordy was mistaken. Just then the two firemen came out of the front door, carrying a body between them. It was a young man in blackened pyjamas. Paramedics moved in swiftly to take over. They examined the victim carefully before fitting an oxygen mask on his face.

The young man was lifted on to a stretcher and the police moved the crowd back so he could be carried to the ambulance. The prone figure somehow managed to lift an arm to wave. Gordy and Suzie were flabbergasted.

'Did you see that?' he said.

'Yes!' she replied, amazed. 'He's *alive*!'

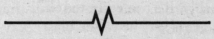

Gilbert Buchanan was a tall, slim, dignified man of sixty with white hair and a goatee beard. He was by far the most eminent surgeon at the hospital and was greatly respected by his colleagues. Though he enjoyed his status, he knew it brought him extra responsibilities. Whenever there was a real emergency in the operating theatre, they usually turned to him.

'I was about to go to bed,' he complained.

'Sorry about that, Gilbert.'

'Thank goodness I didn't have a nightcap! Imagine trying to operate with a whisky and soda inside me!'

'We're just glad to have you here.'

'Good,' said Buchanan with a grin. 'I hate being hauled in at short notice. But it's good to be reminded that the rest of you can't manage without me,' he joked.

Derek Hamill was a plump surgeon in his thirties with a neat moustache. As he strode along the hospital corridor, he began briefing Gilbert Buchanan.

'It's a difficult case,' he said. 'The patient's a young man, a victim of some kind of domestic explosion.'

'You mean, he and his wife had an argument?' Buchanan became serious. 'Ignore my flippancy. Sign of old age. What was it? A gas explosion?'

'Probably. It's too early to tell.'

'How close was he to the blast?'

'Directly above it, from what we can gather. He was asleep in bed. Then the whole house fell about his ears.'

'Oh, dear!'

'The main injuries are to his chest and rib damage may have punctured his lung. And there's severe internal bleeding.'

'Let's not keep him waiting, then.'

They went into the changing room and stripped down to their underpants and socks. After each putting on a pair of clean blue surgical suits, short white boots and a hat, they went into the scrub room. Here, they washed their hands and arms with great thoroughness, put on their face masks, their gowns and their sterile rubber gloves.

Gilbert Buchanan led the way into the operating theatre. His team of assistants was waiting. The patient was already anaesthetized on the table, his naked body covered in lacerations and minor burns. A nurse was bathing some of the surface wounds, but she stepped back when Buchanan came up to the table.

The surgeon conducted his own examination for a few moments then shook his head in sympathy.

'Poor devil!' he said. 'Let's open him up and see the full extent of his injuries.' He looked round at his colleagues.' And brace yourselves, everybody. We could be in for a long night.'

Mark Andrews was the resident TV addict. The four friends he shared the house with each had a favourite programme but Mark was the only one who watched television on a regular basis. As he sat in front of the screen eating a biscuit, he pushed his rimless spectacles up the bridge of his nose. Mark was so absorbed by the late film that he didn't hear the front door.

Gordy and Suzie came into the room.

'Surprise, surprise!' said Gordy with light sarcasm. 'Marco is glued to the box.'

'Hi, Mark,' said Suzie.

He glanced up from the film and gave them a welcoming nod. Then he remembered something and got to his feet.

'Hey, you'll never guess what happened!'

Gordy smirked. 'You were watching the TV.'

'Yes!' said Mark. 'The local news. They had this item about an explosion in Gallagher Road. There was this shot of the house, still smoking. Then they panned across the crowd and I could have sworn I saw you two there.'

'You did,' confirmed Gordy.

'That's why we're so late back,' added Suzie. 'We were driving home from the concert when we heard the bang. The house was in flames when we got there.'

'Wish *I'd* been with you!' said Mark, enviously.

'It was horrible, ' said Suzie.

'I love being where the action is. The main thing is they got the owner out alive and rushed him to hospital.'

'Did they say what his name was?' asked Suzie.

'Yes.' He scratched his head. 'Now, what was it? Um...Stoddard. Yes, that was it. Jamie Stoddard.'

'How serious were his injuries?'

'They didn't give any details, Suzie,' he said. 'It was only a short item. But I *knew* it was you.'

'Fame at last!' said Gordy. 'We're superstars, Suzie.'

'All I can think about is that Mr Stoddard,' she said. 'It's a miracle he came out of that debris in one piece.'

Mark let his vivid imagination take over.

'I bet he's having an emergency op right now,' he said, eyes gleaming. 'Gilbert Buchanan and a number one team. Fighting to save his life. A race against time.'

'Sounds like an episode of *Casualty*,' said Gordie.

'If only I was *there*. Helping to pull him back from the brink. Think of the satisfaction it would give.' Mark smiled wistfully. 'A man is dragged out of a wrecked house with a slim chance of survival. Only a brilliant surgeon can save him.

He and his team battle through the night against the odds. Do you know what he'll say at the end of the operation?'

'Yes,' said Gordy. '"Pass the scalpel, Marco."'

'That would be my dream come true!'

'I just hope Mr Stoddard will pull through,' said Suzie. 'I'm keeping my fingers crossed.'

Mark nodded in agreement. 'Me too.' He switched off the television. 'By the way, how was the concert?'

'Great!' said Gordy. 'Three of the best rock bands in one gig. Even Suzie enjoyed it. I'm trying to wean her off that weird country music. Tonight was a real eye-opener for her, wasn't it, Suze?'

But Suzie wasn't listening to him. She had forgotten all about the pop concert.

Her mind was at the hospital with Jamie Stoddard.

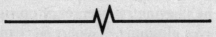

It was well past midnight when the operation was finally over. Gilbert Buchanan's surgical skills had been decisive once again. As the patient was wheeled away, the tension in the operating theatre relaxed. Buchanan pulled down his face mask to reveal a calm smile.

'Well done, everybody!' he said.

'You must take the credit,' noted Derek Hamill. 'The damage to his lung could have been fatal.'

'Not if I could help it,' said Mr Buchanan.

'And he'd lost such a lot of blood.'

'Well, we've stabilized him now. Mr Stoddard was very lucky. And I'm sure you could have done just as good a job yourself, Derek,' said Mr Buchanan, modestly. 'What saved him wasn't my nimble fingers; he had luck on his side.'

'In what way?'

'When the explosion went off, he was under the bedclothes. That gave him some kind of protection. The blast must have hurled him against the wall like a rag doll.'

'That's when he sustained all that rib damage,' suggested Mr Hamill.

'Consider how much worse it would have been if Mr Stoddard had still been downstairs, close to the source of the explosion.'

'He wouldn't have stood a chance!'

'Exactly, Derek. As it is, he's got off with a punctured lung, a broken collarbone, some broken ribs, heavy bruising and some minor burns. Now we've patched him up, he'll soon be on the mend.'

'Well done, Gilbert.'

'It was a team effort. That's what surgery's all about.'

The others muttered their agreement as they left the theatre. Gilbert Buchanan looked round proudly at the operating theatre. There was a sparkle in his eye.

'Another satisfied customer,' he said.

'Mr Stoddard will certainly be grateful to you.'

'I'll pop in first thing in the morning to see how he's getting on. He may be able to hear me better by then.'

'Hear you?' said Hamill.

'Yes, Derek,' said the senior man. 'That blast will have deafened him temporarily. He's lucky it didn't burst his eardrums. This patient obviously leads a charmed life.'

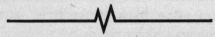

It was a long walk home but Bella Denton was glad of the fresh air. The restaurant had been warm and stuffy. And she wanted an opportunity to stretch her legs.

Halfway home, Damian Holt began to have regrets.

'We should have taken a taxi,' he said.

'It's not that far,' she countered.

'There's almost a mile to go yet.'

'So? We're young, fit and healthy.'

'You haven't been working for ten hours in Casualty,' groaned Damian.

'Stop moaning!' said Bella. 'You've done nothing but complain all night long.'

'Well I'm sorry, but I'm tired.'

'That's one word for it!'

Bella's sharp retort silenced him for a bit. Damian, a doctor at the hospital, was a good-looking young Australian with an eye for the girls and a wicked sense of humour. Bella had liked him from the start. Though he took his work seriously, he had a good sense of fun when he was off duty that fitted in well with her adventurous spirit. Damian had responded to her vivacious good looks as soon as he'd met her.

Their relationship was friendly but erratic. Sometimes Bella went out with other guys but she always came back to Damian in the end. When he'd invited her for a meal tonight, she'd expected the usual good time. But instead, she'd found him in a sombre mood.

'My legs are aching, Bella,' he said.

'Then flag down a taxi and go back to your flat.'

'I must take you home first, Bella.'

'Don't worry,' she said, tartly. 'I can find my own way.'

'You can't walk back alone at this time of night.'

'It can't be any worse than this.'

'Bella!'

'You used to be such fun, Damian.'

He shrugged his shoulders. 'Look, I'm sorry if I've been a bit subdued tonight.'

'Subdued!' she echoed. 'It's like being with a zombie.'

'Ah come on! That's not fair.'

'No, it isn't. Zombies don't whinge all the time.'

Damian bit back a reply and lapsed into silence. He didn't even notice the hospital as it loomed up ahead of them. Usually, they held hands when they were out together – but not this time. They were metres apart.

Though she wasn't enjoying his company tonight, Bella was grateful to have him beside her. She lived in a rough area of the city – bad housing and unemployment kept the crime rate high. There were always gangs of young guys hanging about on street corners. Being alone would have made her an easy target.

When they turned into her road, Bella saw that one of the streetlamps had gone out. She certainly wouldn't have wanted to walk through those shadows on her own. As they came to the dark stretch of pavement, she moved closer to him. Damian took it as a sign of affection and put an arm round her shoulders.

'Sorry, Bella,' he said.

'Forget it.'

'I wasn't at my best tonight. It was a mistake to invite you out.'

'I was the one who made the mistake, Damian.'

'We'll make up for it next time, OK?'

Bella said nothing. But she made up her mind that there would never be a next time. She'd spent almost five hours alone with him and she was bored to death.

They came to the house and stopped in the porch. She moved away from him and his arm fell from her shoulders.

'Good night, Damian,' she said, pointedly.

'Aren't you going to ask me in?'

'No way!'

'Why not?'

'Because I've had enough.'

Damian looked hurt but, recovering quickly, he flashed her one of his famous grins and pointed to the living room.

'The light's out,' he observed. 'The others have all gone to bed. If you invited me in, we'd be alone.'

'That's what I'm worried about,' said Bella. 'Look, we've had a terrible night,' she said, reasonably. 'Let's just accept that and call it a day.'

'I thought it was quite a good meal.'

'The meal was fine – the conversation wasn't.'

'I told you – I'd had a hard day in Casualty.'

'In that case you should have enjoyed letting yourself go this evening. Not just curl up like a wet lettuce.'

Anger made Bella's face glow. He tried another tack.

'Let me in and I'll apologise.'

'It's too late for that, Damian.'

He moved closer to her. 'How about a kiss to make friends.'

'Oh, no!' she said, pushing him away.

'Come on, Bella,' he said. 'What's got into you?'

'Terminal fatigue.'

'You were the one who insisted on walking home.'

'It's not physical fatigue, Damian. I feel fine in myself. What's dying on its feet is our relationship.'

'But we've had great times together!'

'Yes – in the past,' she said.

'And we will again.'

'No, Damian. Find someone else to moan about Casualty to. I've had an earful. Do you think being a student nurse is a rest cure? Because it isn't, I can tell you. We work our socks off. But did *I* complain that I'd had a tough day at the hospital?'

'Well – no.'

'Because I put it all behind me. I just wanted a couple of hours of relaxation with Dr Damian Holt and his famous bedside manner.'

'I've said I'm sorry. What more can I do?'

'Go home.'

'Don't I even get a kiss?'

'Go home and don't bother to call me.'

'But I want to see you again.'

'Not if I see you first.'

Damian was surprised. He'd never seen Bella so angry.

'Are you saying that...we're finished?'

'Yes,' she told him, opening the front door with her key. 'In a word – goodbye!'

And she shut the door firmly in his face.

—√— CHAPTER THREE —√—

Karlene Smith had never regretted her decision to become a physiotherapist. The course was difficult and her hours were long but she loved the work. Karlene derived a great deal of help and moral support from her tutor, Catherine White. She had become a real friend and inspiration.

'Good morning, Karlene.'

'Hello, Mrs White.'

'You're always the first one here.'

'I like to make an early start.'

'I wish everyone had that attitude.'

'The truth is, if I didn't get up at the crack of dawn, I'd never get in the bathroom,' admitted Karlene.

Her tutor laughed. 'Sharing a house does have its problems.'

'Five of us, fighting over one bathroom,' groaned Karlene.

'The end result is the same, you get to the hospital before anyone else on the course.'

Catherine White was a tall, thin, elegant woman whose dark hair was streaked with grey. Wearing a white coat, she was sitting behind the desk in her office. Karlene was standing opposite her. Her tutor consulted a piece of paper in front of her.

'I've got you down for observation this afternoon.'

'Good,' said Karlene. 'I can look and learn.'

'That's the idea. If you watch us working with a group of patients, you can see the techniques we use. Those techniques may very slightly with each individual.'

'How do you know which one to choose?'

'Experience and instinct,' said Mrs White. 'You'll have no problems,' she continued. 'You're an intuitive person. That's why you'll be an excellent physio one day.'

'I hope so.'

'We're working with a group of amputees this afternoon – they're a fairly mixed bunch of people. Some have come to terms with their disability and some have not. Some work with us, and some resist.' She glanced down at her piece of paper. 'Pay particular attention to Daisy Collier. She's a young girl – only ten years old.'

'What's happened to her?'

'Daisy's leg was crushed when she jumped from a moving bus. There was no way to save it. The surgeon had to amputate the lower half of the limb.'

'Poor girl!' Karlene felt shocked.

'Yes, she's still rather traumatized by it all.'

'I can imagine.'

'Keep a special eye on her, will you, Karlene?' Catherine White sighed, then smiled gravely.

'Why?'

'You'll see, Karlene. You'll understand when you meet her.'

Student nurses at the hospital didn't spend all their time in lectures or in libraries; practical experience was a vital part of their course. It was very often thrust upon them at short notice. Today, Bella was unhappy about the situation.

'Why does Sister Killeen always pick on us?' she complained.

'Who cares?' replied Mark. 'I'm just grateful that we get so much hands-on experience.'

'Yes – hands on dirty sheets, hands on bedpans.'

'We have to start at the bottom, Bella.'

They laughed at his unintentional pun. Then they got into the lift in the main block and went up to the fourth floor. Sister Killeen was their tutor and she usually gave them a joint assignment. There were always staff shortages at the hospital and student nurses filled the gaps.

'I thought you liked escaping from Sister Killeen,' he said.

'I do, Mark.'

'So why are you complaining now?'

'Because I don't really want to be in the main block.'

'But this is where it all the action is, Bella.'

'I know!' she said, gloomily. 'It also happens to be the place where Damian works.'

'Damian Holt?'

'I want to avoid him at all costs.'

'But I thought it was on again,' said Mark. 'Didn't he take you out for a meal a couple of nights ago?'

'That's what finished him.'

'You mean, it's off again?'

'Permanently.'

Mark didn't comment. Bella's romantic entanglements were a constant mystery to him. He had never known anyone attract and discard so many boyfriends in such a short time.

The lift stopped and they stepped out on the fourth floor. A large sign directed them to Mendip Ward at the back of the building. Sister Judd was there, waiting to greet them.

'Hurry along there,' she chided. 'I've got work for you.'

Sister Judd was an unusually tall, big-boned woman. She towered over them but though rather intimidating, her manner was friendly. She showed the newcomers round and outlined their duties.

Mendip Ward was divided into three open bays, each containing six beds. It also had four single cubicles for infectious patients. At the far end of the ward was a small day-room and beyond it was another unit.

'What's through there, Sister Judd?' asked Mark, pointing at the double doors.

'Nothing that need concern you,' she replied. 'It's a separate unit – for private patients.'

Bella was surprised. 'But this is an NHS hospital. I didn't know we had private patients in here.'

'Only a very small number. As it happens, just one room in the unit is taken at the moment.'

Mark peered through the glass panel in the door and read the name on the first room. His curiosity was aroused.

'Stoddard!' he said. 'Wasn't that the chap caught in the explosion the other night?'

'Yes,' said Sister Judd. 'But you won't be seeing anything of him. Mr Stoddard is a private patient. You will only be dealing with National Health admissions.'

'How is he?' asked Bella.

'He's making good progress.'

'Gordy and Suzie, two friends of ours, were there,' explained Mark.

'Yes,' added Bella. 'They were close to the house when it exploded. They rushed straight to the scene and Suzie's dying to know how Mr Stoddard is getting on.'

Sister Judd was brisk. 'As I said, he's making progress. And that's something you two must start to do.'

She brushed aside further questions about Jamie Stoddard and sent them off about their duties. Both of them worked well but they kept glancing at the private unit. Why was the patient alone in there? It gave him an element of mystery that was quite intriguing.

But they had to wait until mid-afternoon to learn more about him. Bella and Mark were stripping a bed at the far end of the ward.

'He demanded a private room,' she said.

'Who, Mr Stoddard?'

'Yes. One of the nurses just told me. They'd put him in a cubicle in a general ward but he didn't like that at all. He insisted on being completely alone.'

'That means he has money. Perhaps he's in one of those schemes,' decided Mark. 'In any case, he must be well off to live in Gallagher Road. And Gordy told us he had a Mercedes in the garage.'

'Young and wealthy!' said Bella. 'Just my type! And I don't think he's married or he wouldn't have been alone in the house.'

Mark grinned. 'You're incorrigible, Bella!'

Footsteps approached and they looked up to see Gilbert Buchanan marching down the ward with a nurse in attendance. He gave Mark and Bella a genial smile then pushed open the door of the private unit. He and his companion vanished into the room occupied by Jamie

Stoddard.

Mark was impressed. 'Did you see who that was!'

'Gilbert Buchanan.'

'He's the best surgeon in the hospital.'

'Yes,' said Bella, smiling. 'If Mr Stoddard can afford to pay for *his* services, he must be rolling in it!'

'Don't be so mercenary.'

'I'm showing a nurse's natural interest in a patient,' she said.

When the bed was stripped, Mark took the old sheets off to the laundry and Bella began to make the bed with clean linen, taking her time so that she could keep one eye on the private unit. Her patience was rewarded.

The nurse came out of the private unit and held the door open for Gilbert Buchanan. He had paused to say a few last words to the patient and Bella was at a perfect angle to see into the private room and get a glimpse of Jamie Stoddard. A bright smile lit up her face.

The patient was handsome, dark-haired and in his early twenties. Sitting up in bed, he had his arm in a sling and a saline drip attached to his other wrist. But his face seemed to be remarkably unmarked by the explosion.

As the surgeon was about to leave, Jamie Stoddard caught Bella's eye. Surprised to find himself under surveillance, he was quick to note her attractive face and good figure. In that brief moment, a bond was established between them.

He winked at her. Bella smiled back with pleasure.

—————✻—————

Karlene spotted her at once. Daisy Collier was a pretty girl with curly brown hair brushed back from her face and held in a blue scrunchie. She was wearing a denim dress. The room was large and well-equipped and three physiotherapists were working under the guidance of Catherine White. All the patients had suffered amputations and were being taught to strengthen their surviving limbs to get maximum use from them.

Helped out of her wheelchair, Daisy was being shown how to get used to her crutches. She was not the most easy of patients. There was a deep scowl on her face.

Mrs White slipped across to Karlene.

'Can you see our problem?' asked her tutor. 'She's not speaking to anyone.'

'We just can't coax her out of her shell.'

'Did you say she jumped from a moving bus?'

'There was a bit more to it than that, I believe, but Daisy won't even talk about it. Neither will her mother.'

'How often will Daisy be in here?'

'She comes every afternoon.'

'Do you think that *I* could speak to her, Mrs

33

White?'

'Certainly,' she said. 'But don't expect an answer. The poor girl has really gone into herself.'

Karlene bided her time. She waited until Daisy had been through her exercise programe before walking across to her. She was hunched up in her wheelchair again.

'Hello,' said Karlene. 'How are you getting along?'

Daisy gave her a resentful glare.

'I'm Karlene,' she persisted, 'I'm training to be a physio.'

But her friendly smile elicited no word from Daisy.

'I daresay you're fed up with physios, Daisy. We're terrible people. We make patients get out of bed and do exercises when they just want to rest. Maybe that's why you don't like us? Because we keep trying to make you do things?'

Karlene's jokey manner was getting nowhere. She knelt down in front of Daisy and tried a more serious tone.

'We're all really sorry about what happened to you,' she said. 'It was such terrible luck – but life is like that sometimes. You've just got to fight back, Daisy. We're here to help you do just that. Mrs White – she's my tutor – is the most brilliant physio. You can really trust her. She's dealt with loads of cases just like yours. She'll have you up and about in no time at all.'

Daisy lowered her head and stared at the ground.

'I'll see you in here tomorrow. OK?'

Daisy looked up and shook her head vigorously.

'Why not?' asked Karlene.

'Because I don't want to, that's why!'

Daisy swung her wheelchair round and propelled herself quickly towards the exit. Karlene sighed. Catherine White came across to talk to her.

'Did you manage to make her speak?'

'Yes,' said Karlene, ruefully. 'But I wish I hadn't now. Daisy's full of pent-up anger. Why do you think?'

Suzie didn't realize there was so much to learn about radiography. The work was interesting but very intensive and it put a lot of pressure on her. It was a relief when she was given a fairly ordinary task. She was asked to take a set of x-rays across to Casualty and it gave her a brief break in an otherwise very busy day.

On her way over, she bumped into a familiar figure.

'Hi, Damian!' she said.

'Oh...hi, Suzie.'

'I haven't seen you for ages.'

'It's been pretty busy over here.'

Dr Damian Holt seemed rather embarrassed. He'd always liked Suzie and they'd had some long chats about her work at the hospital, but his real friendship was with Bella. But now he feared that was a thing of the past.

'Has Bella...said anything to you?' he asked. 'About me and her?'

'Not a word,' said Suzie.

'We're splitting up.'

'Oh really? I'm sorry.'

'To be honest, she gave me the push.'

'Don't take that too seriously,' advised Suzie. 'Bella tends to say crazy things in the heat of the moment.'

'She meant it, Suzie. No doubt about that.'

'You know Bella – she always blows hot and cold.'

'I got the cool treatment the other night,' he said with a painful grin. 'But I suppose I deserved it.'

'I shouldn't think so, Damian. You took her out for a delicious meal. She should have been pleased.'

Damian was grateful to her. Suzie obviously knew the whole story but was being tactful to protect his feelings. He admired that. Of the three girls in the house, Suzie was always the most diplomatic.

'Maybe it's a good thing,' he said. 'We both need some breathing space.'

'You said that the last time.'

'Yes,' he agreed with a smile. 'And the time before that, I know. It's a repeating pattern. But it's different this time, Suzie. She's really choked off with me.'

'She'll come round in time.'

'But I don't know that I want her to come round.'

'What do you mean?'

'I shouldn't have asked her out the other night. Bella's a fun girl. If you take her out, she expects some real action. Parties, discos, excitement. That's her scene. She's not really good at doling out the sympathy.'

'Why do you need sympathy, Damian?'

'It doesn't matter now.' He looked sad.

'But it does,' she said, seriously. 'Friendship isn't always about dancing the night away. It has other sides, too.'

'*You* understand that, Suzie – but Bella doesn't.'

'Would you like me to speak to her?'

'No, no!' he said, quickly. 'I'd rather let the whole thing cool off. Who knows, perhaps we'll drift back together one day? When it's all sorted out.'

'When what's sorted out?'

'Oh nothing. I won't burden you with my problems.'

'They're not a burden, Damian. I'd like to help.'

'Perhaps I should have taken you out for dinner instead.'

'That would have gone down well with Bella!'

They laughed – but she could tell he was still upset about something. His normal, easy-going manner had been replaced by an uncertainty. Dr Damian Holt was clearly under a lot of strain. Suzie was concerned.

'I meant what I said just now, Damian. If there's anything I can do to help...'

'This isn't really the time or the place,' he said, nodding to a colleague who went past. 'It's better if you deliver your x-rays and forget all about what I've said.'

'But I can't. We're *friends*, aren't we?'

'I'd like to think so, Suzie.'

'Then rely on me for sympathy if you need it.'

'That's very kind of you,' said Damian.

'So – shall we have a chat some time?'

He hesitated. 'Well...'

'I'm not trying to pry, Damian. If you don't want to confide in me, don't worry. But if you ever need a shoulder to cry on...'

'That's what I hoped Bella would provide.'

Damian was clearly pleased by her offer of sympathy but he wasn't yet ready to commit himself. He glanced at his watch and muttered something about being late for an appointment.

'Do you want to meet up away from the hospital?' she suggested.

'Let me think about it, Suzie.'

'Right – you know where to find me.'

He nodded grimly and trudged off down the corridor.

———————∧∨———————

Gordy was talking through a mouthful of hamburger.

'What's her name?' he asked.

'Daisy Collier,' said Karlene.

'And she refuses to speak to anyone?'

'I didn't make any headway at all. Until the end. Then she more or less told me to push off.'

'Charming!'

'It was no worse than watching you eat a hamburger,' she teased. 'Could you possibly eat with your mouth shut, Gordy?'

'It's like leather,' he argued. 'I have to chew it like this.'

They were having lunch together in the hospital canteen. Karlene was due to meet Daisy again that afternoon and she wasn't looking forward to it. She didn't feel confident. Gordy offered her his advice.

'She's probably still traumatized by the accident,' he suggested. 'It's still haunting her and she's trying to come to terms with losing half her leg. That's why she's retreated into a private world. She just needs time to adjust, I'm sure.'

'I hope you're right. I hope it's nothing more sinister.'

'I am, Kar. Doctor Robbins has diagnosed the problem.'

'Even though you've never met Daisy?'

'Well, you've given me a full case history.'

'But I haven't, Gordy,' she said. 'That's the problem. There's something missing – no one knows the details of the accident which caused Daisy to lose her leg. If I knew exactly what happened, I might be able to understand her. But right now, it's like getting blood out of a stone.'

As Gordy started to attack his hamburger again, Mark came over to join them. Putting his plate of salad on the table, he lowered himself into a chair.

'How's it all going with you guys?' he asked.

'It's not,' said Gordy, mid-chew. 'Kar has got a patient who won't speak to her and they've given me the toughest hamburger in captivity. I need a laser beam to cut through this!'

Suzie couldn't bear to watch Gordy any longer. 'Where's Bella?' she said, turning to Mark. 'I thought she was coming over for lunch.'

'A change of plan,' explained Mark. 'Jamie Stoddard.'

'The patient hurt in the explosion?'

'That's right. I told you, he has a private room at the end of Mendip Ward. Sister Judd warned us to keep well away from it because he doesn't want any visitors. But you know Bella. Once her interest in a man is aroused, there's no stopping her.'

'He must be in a dreadful condition,' said Gordy. 'We saw him being carried out on a stretcher.'

'He's making a good recovery, apparently. And now Bella has decided that she should be part of his recovery. She's a law unto herself.'

'Surely Bella realizes she mustn't get involved with one of the patients?'

'Sister Killeen has tried to drum that into us, yes.'

Gordy sighed. 'Bella obviously didn't hear the drum.'

'She's wasting her time,' said Suzie. 'How on earth can she get to him if he's a private patient?'

'Bella will find a way,' said Mark. 'Somehow.'

Bella made a good impression on the patients in Mendip Ward. She was bright, cheerful and efficient. In the short time she'd been there, she'd got to know all their names and always had a moment for a brief chat. She'd also befriended the patients in the cubicles at the end of the ward. While she waited for an opportunity to slip into the private unit, she put her head round the door of one of the cubicles.

'How are you today, Mrs Lassiter?' she asked.

'A little better,' said the old lady in the bed.

'We'll have you up and about in no time at all.'

'I hope so.'

'Anything you need?'

'Not just now, dear.'

'I'll drop in again later.'

'Thank you, Nurse.'

Bella shut one door and saw her chance to sneak unobserved through another. She darted into the private unit and paused outside the first room. She straightened her uniform and adjusted her hair and, tapping on the door, she went straight in.

Jamie Stoddard was propped up in bed reading

a newspaper. He seemed annoyed at the interruption.

'Yes, who are you?' he asked, sharply.

'Bella,' she said. 'Bella Denton. I'm a student nurse here.'

'You're not assigned to this room, are you?'

'Er, well...no, I suppose I'm not.'

'So what are you doing here?'

'I just wondered if there was anything I could get you.'

'Complete privacy – that's all I need.'

'Oh yes. Of course.'

Looking crestfallen, Bella started to back out of the room.

'Hang on a minute,' he said, studying her more closely.

'Sorry, I shouldn't have barged in, Mr Stoddard.'

'Haven't I seen you somewhere before?'

'Only for a second,' she said. 'You winked at me through the open door.'

'Ah, that was you, was it?' He relaxed a little. 'So we're already acquainted. What's your name again?'

'Bella.'

'Nice to meet you, Bella. I'm Jamie.'

He put his paper on one side and smiled warmly at her. Bella was able to get a good look at him for the first time. He was young and slim, with an open face. His voice was pleasant and, as he ran his eye over her figure, he clearly liked what he saw.

'Why not tell me the truth?' he suggested. 'You didn't really drop in on the off-chance that I needed something, did you? You had another reason.' He smiled at her. 'Come on, Bella. What brought you here?'

'Suzie and Gordy.'

'Who on earth are they?'

'They're friends of mine. Suzie's a trainee radiodog and Gordy is in the medical school here. They've got a personal interest in your case.'

He looked guarded. 'Have they? Why?'

'They were driving home the other night when they heard this huge explosion. They got to your house just in time to see you being brought out.' She stepped closer to him. 'It must have been a horrifying experience for you.'

'I don't really remember much about it.'

'Did you just black out?'

'Sort of. It all happened so suddenly.'

'You survived, that's the main thing. Considering the force of the explosion, you've been very lucky. Apart from that bruise on your forehead, your face is unmarked.'

'I've always been lucky, Bella.'

'I should sue them for every penny they've got – the gas board, that is. If it was their fault.'

'We'll have to see about that.'

'If I was in your position—'

'Look, Bella,' he said, cutting her off, 'do you mind if we don't talk about the accident? It's rather a painful subject. I just want to rest and recuperate.'

'That's why I came, really,' she confessed. 'To see how you were getting on. Suzie and Gordy want to keep track of your condition. Now I can tell them that you look great.'

'I will do, when my injuries begin to heal.'

He gave her an open and admiring smile. She responded with a grin as he winked at her again. Then Bella became inquisitive.

'You don't seem to have many visitors,' she noted.

'I don't have any – by choice.'

'What about your family?'

'They live abroad.'

'Didn't they want to fly back and see you when they heard the news about the explosion?'

'No, Bella,' he explained, 'because they don't know anything about the accident. And I don't want to alarm them.'

'But people need their families around them at times like these,' she argued. 'I know I would.'

'We've never been all that close. And my mother has enough anxieties as it is – I didn't want to add to them. When I'm back on my feet again, I'll call them and tell them the whole story.'

'That's very considerate.'

'It works both ways. They don't get into a state about me – and I don't have to cope with them being here. As I told you, I value my privacy.'

'Does that mean *nobody*'s allowed in here?'

'Nobody – apart from Mr Buchanan and the nurse on duty.'

'In that case, I'll get out of your way.'

'There is one exception to the rule – as long as you know how to be discreet.'

'Me?' she asked, delighted.

'But I don't want you talking about me.'

'I won't say anything, Mr Stoddard.'

'Jamie,' he corrected.

She smiled at him. 'Jamie,' she repeated.

'Are you *sure* I can trust you, Bella?'

'Quite sure,' she said, firmly.

Jamie Stoddard studied her for what seemed like an age before coming to a decision. He nodded.

'I could use a friend in this place,' he said, easily. 'Will you come and see me again, Bella?'

'Oh yes,' she promised. 'Absolutely!'

By the third afternoon, Karlene felt she was starting to make a breakthrough. Daisy actually smiled at her. It was a grudging smile, but it marked a big step forward. At their first meeting, she had been silent and resentful with Karlene, and on the second day, Karlene found Daisy retreating even further into her shell. But, on the following afternoon, in response to a cheery wave from Karlene, Daisy actually managed a smile.

Karlene went quickly over to her.

'Hi, Daisy,' she said, with a welcoming grin.

'Hello,' she replied, warily.

'How are you feeling today?'

'Not too bad.'

'Great! That's great. Have you done all your exercises?'

'Yes.'

'And you're building up your strength, little by little, every day.'

'So – what's the point?'

'To make you independent,' said Karlene. 'You don't want to spend the rest of your life in a wheelchair, do you?'

Daisy shrugged. She looked bleakly at Karlene.

The room was full of activity. Catherine White and the other physiotherapists were working with the patients, taking them through their exercises and encouraging them to reach the targets that had been set.

One patient, a factory worker who had lost his right arm in an industrial accident, was learning how to develop his skill with his left arm. And a woman whose leg had been amputated was trying out her artificial limb with the aid of a zimmer frame. All the other patients were fighting hard to overcome their various handicaps.

Daisy seemed the odd one out. She had no urge to fight. She appeared resigned and depressed and Karlene was determined to help her overcome her feelings.

'Have your friends been to see you?' she asked.

'Some of them...' Daisy began.

'I bet they were jealous.'

'Why should they be jealous?'

'Because of all the schoolwork you're missing.'

The small smile again appeared. 'Maybe.'

'Do you like school, Daisy?'

'No way!'

'Neither did I. I couldn't wait to leave.'

'It's so boring most of the time, it sends me to sleep.'

'You must have *some* good teachers.'

'Oh – one or two.'

'Who's your favourite?'

'Miss Whitlow,' said Daisy, spontaneously, showing a hint of enthusiasm at last. 'She's great! We always have a good laugh with Miss Whitlow. She's not like the others. She understands us.'

'What does she teach?'

'Games.'

Her smile froze. Daisy suddenly realized that she would never be able to take part in a games lesson with her favourite teacher again. The sense of loss made her gasp. Karlene put a hand on her arm.

'What do you want to be, Daisy? When you leave school?'

Daisy shrugged again.

'You must have some idea. At your age, I knew exactly what career I was going to choose,' said Karlene. 'I was going to be a supermodel. One of those gorgeous girls you see on the front of magazines. Crazy, wasn't it? I could never be a model in a million years – but that was my dream.'

'So what happened?'

'I got interested in this job instead.'

'*Do* you like it?' Daisy's interest began to flicker.

'I love it. I'm doing something useful and I meet lots of interesting people – like you.'

Daisy's mouth twitched but no smile came. She was still thinking about Miss Whitlow and the games lessons. A huge sense of loss descended on her – school would be even more boring now.

Karlene felt deeply sorry for Daisy. She wanted to offer her support but she couldn't do that until she knew the full story of her accident. She leaned closer to her.

'What actually happened, Daisy?' she whispered.

'Happened?'

'On that bus – when you jumped off.'

Daisy started as though she'd been struck across the face.

'Why won't you tell me about it?' continued Karlene. 'You'll have to come to terms with it sooner or later.'

'Just leave me alone,' said Daisy, quietly.

'I'm trying to help you.'

'I don't *need* your help.'

'Daisy, I'm on your side.'

'Go away.'

'Don't shut me out Daisy,' persisted Karlene.

'Go away!' she shouted. 'Go away! Go away!'

Everybody in the room had stopped to look at them. Karlene felt deeply embarrassed – and Daisy burst into tears.

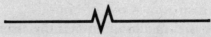

'You never learn, do you, Bella?' said Mark.

'What do you mean?'

'Sister Judd told you to stay away from that room.'

'And I do,' said Bella. 'Most of the time.'

'Can't you just leave Mr Stoddard alone?'

'But I like talking to him.'

'Bella, he's a private patient – he's no concern of ours.'

'He is now – Jamie's a friend.'

'You're asking for trouble, Bella.'

'What harm is there in having an occasional chat with him?'

'A lot of harm – if Sister Judd catches you.'

'She won't, Mark. I'm very careful.'

'I'd hate to see you get into trouble.'

'Then you can act as my look-out while I'm in Jamie's room. If anyone heads for the private unit, come and tell me.'

Mark and Bella had enjoyed a late lunch together before strolling back towards Mendip Ward. They'd settled into a routine there and Mark was enjoying it. He didn't want Bella's behaviour to threaten their position on the ward.

'You went in there again this morning,' he reminded her.

'Only for a few minutes. Jamie was really pleased to see me.'

'Bella, his room is out of bounds.'

'Not to me – he more or less invited me in.'

'It's just too risky,' Mark replied, looking serious.

'That's the attraction.' She smiled happily. 'Actually, I feel sorry for him, Mark. He lost everything in that explosion. But he doesn't seem at all upset by what he's lost – he's just grateful he survived.'

'So he should be.'

'He's such an interesting guy.'

'You don't know anything about him. You told me yesterday how secretive he was. You don't even know what he does for a living.'

'Something to do with banking, I think.'

'Is that what he told you?'

'Well, not exactly.'

'So it's just a wild guess.'

'No,' she argued. 'I worked it out. All the other patients take newspapers like the *Sun* or the *Daily Mirror*. Not Jamie Stoddard.'

'What does he read?'

'The *Financial Times*.'

Mark was intrigued. 'That *is* unusual.'

'When I was in there this morning, he mentioned something about stocks and shares.'

'Perhaps he's a stockbroker.'

'No, Mark. A banker. I have this gut feeling. My guess is that he's a manager somewhere.'

'He's far too young for that.'

'But he's really clever – you can tell that by talking to him. He seems to have a gift for figures.' She smiled again and smoothed down her uniform. 'That's why he admires mine.'

Mark decided not to comment, but he still had nagging doubts. There were too many things about Jamie Stoddard that didn't add up. It worried him that Bella was getting involved so easily with this patient.

'Listen,' he said, 'I don't want to sound like Sister Killeen...'

'You already do.'

'But nurses must never get too close to patients.'

'I've only had a couple of chats with him.'

'But one thing leads to another.'

'When he's got a broken collarbone and one arm in plaster? It's not like that, Mark. We're just friends.'

'But why? There are other nurses in Mendip Ward. And he has his own private nurse to look after him. Not to mention Gilbert Buchanan. Why doesn't he befriend them?'

'Because we have something special between us.'

'Oh yeah – what's that, Bella?'

'We just get along, that's all.'

'As long as he doesn't use you.'

'Mark!'

'Well, I don't want him taking advantage.'

'Jamie isn't like that,' she assured him. 'He's kind and considerate. He won't even tell his parents he's in hospital because it will upset them too much.'

Mark bit back his advice – it was wasted on Bella. She didn't want to hear any criticism of Jamie Stoddard. He was her friend now and she was enjoying the relationship.

'It's wonderful!' she said. 'Jamie is such a private man yet he's allowed one person close to him – me! I feel honoured. I'm really getting to know him now, better than anybody else.

They had just reached Mendip Ward when they both got a shock. Jamie Stoddard was being wheeled towards them on a trolley. A doctor was by his side and he was covered with a blanket and seemed to be in pain. Bella was horrified as the trolley was pushed past her. She turned to Sister Judd who was walking behind Jamie.

'What's happened to him, Sister?'

'Mr Stoddard ignored medical advice,' she said, grimly. 'He was so anxious to leave, he tried to get out of bed and discharge himself from hospital. Some of his stitches ripped open and he's being rushed off to have them repaired.' Sister Judd looked after the trolley. 'He hates being in here. For some reason, Mr Stoddard can't *wait* to get out of the place.'

Bella felt rather stupid. Her boast sounded hollow now. She really didn't know Jamie Stoddard as well as she'd imagined.

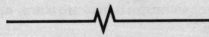

Gordy was dusting his skeleton, Matilda, when there was a gentle knock on the door.

'Come on in, Suze!' he called.

Suzie pushed open the door to his room.

'How did you know it was me?' she asked, baffled.

'By the gentle tap. Kar thumps it, Marco gives it a sharp rap and Bella just barges in without even bothering to knock. It had to be you.'

Suzie looked at the skeleton suspended from a hook.

'Are you giving Matilda a spring-clean.'

'Yes,' he said, rubbing her skull. 'She gets very dusty.' He stood back to admire his handiwork. 'That'll do, Matilda. You look as good as new.'

He turned to Suzie and whistled approvingly.

'Wow! You really are dressed up.'

'I wondered if you could zip me up, please.'

'My pleasure,' he said, standing behind her to pull the zip of her blue dress up to her neck. 'Who's the lucky guy?'

'There isn't one, Gordy.'

'You mean, you've put on your best gear for a *girl*?'

'These are not my best clothes,' said Suzie, laughing. 'This is one of my oldest dresses. You're so used to seeing me around the house in jeans and a sweatshirt that anything else looks glamorous.'

'You always look glamorous to me, Suze,' he said, gallantly. 'Even in a boiler suit, you'd look pretty terrific.'

'Thanks, Gordy.'

He beamed at her. Suzie was fond of him but resisted all his offers to take her out. It was a rule of the house that there would be no serious relationships between any of them. Suzie believed it would upset the balance completely. Besides, she felt more like a sister to Gordy than anything else.

'I repeat,' he said. 'Who is he?'

'Dr Damian Holt.'

He was amazed. 'You're going out with Damian!'

'No – not in the way you mean.'

'But you are seeing him tonight?'

'Only for a drink.'

'It usually starts that way.

'Gordy!'

'Well, he is up for grabs now, Suze. Bel ditched him again. Jump in while you can.'

'That's a dreadful thing to say!'

'All's fair in love and war.'

'This has nothing to do with love,' she insisted. 'I like Damian but he could never be more than a friend. We decided to have a drink together, that's all. It's not a crime, is it?'

'Of course not.'

'Then no more jokes, please.'

'Sorry, Suze. I'm only jealous of Dr Damian. I'd give my eyeteeth to take you out for an evening. My love life has been a disaster lately.'

He pointed to his skeleton. 'Here's *my* regular date – Matilda.'

'I keep telling you, I am not going on a date.'

'In that case you won't mind me mentioning it to Bel.'

Suzie hesitated. 'No,' she decided. 'Better not. She might get hold of the wrong end of the stick.'

'If she's finished with her Aussie admirer, why should she care who goes out with him?'

'Don't say a word, just to be on the safe side.'

'Is that a request?'

'It's an order, Gordy.'

'So there *is* something between you and Damian?'

'For the last time,' emphasized Suzie, 'the answer is a big NO. Not now, not ever. We need to...discuss something, that's all. And I don't want Bella to know that we've even met. Is that OK?'

'My lips are sealed, Suze.'

'Good.' She kissed him on the cheek. 'Keep them that way. It will save us all a lot of upset.'

Smiling, she let herself out of his room.

CHAPTER SIX

Damian was waiting for Suzie at the White Unicorn. The pub was within easy walking distance of the hospital. Because it got crowded later on, they had arranged to meet early and Damian had managed to find a table in a quiet corner.

When Suzie arrived, she saw how exhausted he looked. Working in Casualty was very tiring but it didn't usually leave Damian so low. There was a defensive look about him as he glanced nervously around, as if he was wondering where the next blow would come from.

When he saw Suzie, his depression lifted for a moment.

'Hi, Suzie,' he welcomed. 'You look great.'

'Thanks.' She sat beside him. 'How are you?'

'Worn out.' He pointed to the half-empty glass of beer on the table. 'Hope you don't mind. I started without you.'

'No problem,' she said, calmly.

He bought Suzie a glass of white wine and then they compared notes about their respective days at the hospital. She talked eagerly as usual, but Damian seemed distracted. Suzie gave him time to relax before she changed the conversation.

'I'm so glad you got in touch with me,

Damian. And I meant what I said – I'm here to help.'

'Thanks.' He sipped his drink. 'Does Bella know we're meeting like this?'

'Of course not.'

'Good.'

'She'd only jump to conclusions.'

'We don't want that to happen,' he added, morosely.

Damian lapsed into silence and was staring into his beer. Suzie waited for a while before she prompted him.

'Well?' There was no response. 'Damian!'

He came out of his trance. 'What...? Oh, sorry. I was miles away. Kick me hard next time I do that.'

'You look as if you've taken enough kicks already.'

'You're so right, Suzie!' he said with feeling. 'I feel sore all over, believe me.'

'Why's that?'

'Because of this...problem I have.'

'Do you want to tell me about it?'

He nodded. 'I certainly need to tell somebody.'

'Is it about money?'

'Indirectly.'

'Is it tied up with hospital politics?'

'In a way. It's a medical problem, Suzie.'

'Medical?' She was worried. 'You're not ill, are you?'

'Not at the moment,' he said wearily, 'but it's only a matter of time. This whole business is like a wasting disease.'

'What exactly *has* happened?' Suzie persisted.

Damian took a deep breath and started to tell her.

'I have to appear before a Board of Inquiry at the hospital, Suzie. If they find me guilty, there's a strong chance I'll lose my job and get kicked out.'

———————⋀———————

Bella remained at the hospital well into the evening. She was desperate for news about Jamie Stoddard. When he was taken back to his room off Mendip Ward, she was kept away by Sister Judd. It was hours before she finally had the opportunity to slip into the private unit.

Jamie was propped up in bed as before. But instead of reading, he was staring ruefully in front of him. As Bella knocked and came in, he shrank back for a second.

'Oh, it's you,' he said with a faint smile.

'Am I disturbing you?'

'No, no. Come on in, Bella.'

'I just had to find out how you were.'

'Disgusted with myself. I must have been mad to try to walk out of here. Mr Buchanan warned me I'd need to stay for at least a week. But I thought I knew better - and now look what's happened!'

'You looked as though you were in pain when they took you to surgery.'

'It was agony, Bella. But I guess it serves me right.'

'I expect you got bored being cooped up in here, that's all.'

'It's a bit worse than being bored.' He looked round the room, then slapped the bed angrily. 'I must get out of here soon!' he said through gritted teeth.

'But only when you're fully recovered.'

'I could check into a hotel – I could get all the bed-rest I need there. And I wouldn't feel so shut in.'

He beckoned Bella across to him and asked her to sit beside the bed. Jamie stared deep into her eyes as if searching for something. Bella was excited to be so close to him, but a little uneasy under his intense stare.

'Can I really trust you, Bella?' he said, finally.

'Of course you can.'

'You wouldn't let me down, would you?'

'We're friends, aren't we?'

'That's what I hoped you'd say.'

'I'd do anything to help you if you asked me,' said Bella. 'Anything!' she vowed.

'And no questions asked?'

'If that's the way you want it – no questions.'

'I thought I could rely on you, Bella.'

She was thrilled with the idea that Jamie would

trust her enough to carry out some kind of mission on his behalf. She grinned happily and leaned close to him.

'What do you want me to do, Jamie?' she asked.

'Nothing at the moment. But I might need you in reserve.'

'Just say the word.'

'Thank you,' he said, quietly. 'Because I may need to ask you a favour. A very big favour.'

———————⋀———————

'When did all this happen?' asked a very attentive Suzie.

'During my first week in Casualty.'

'That's really bad luck!'

'It was a Saturday night,' said Damian. 'The place was a madhouse. Every seat was occupied and emergencies were being brought in constantly. I really don't know how we got through that night.'

'It's the kind of situation that appeals to Mark,' she said, smiling.

'Wait until he tries it, Suzie. When there's an endless queue of patients, you feel overwhelmed. You know you can't give each one the full attention they need.'

'But you did your best in this case, Damian.'

'It wasn't good enough.' He pursed his lips and shook his head. 'The kid had fallen off his bike and banged his head, so they rushed him into us. I dressed the wounds on his face and arms and then sent him off for a cranial x-ray. There seemed to be no serious damage.'

'No sign of a fracture?'

'None whatsoever. As he was still concussed, I made him spend the night in hospital – for observation. They discharged him the next day and I thought that was that.'

'And wasn't it?'

'No, Suzie. The boy started to complain of pains in his ribs. So his father brought him back for more x-rays – and what do you think they found?' Damian looked grim. 'Hairline fractures to three ribs and a more serious crack on a fourth. Goodness knows why he hadn't complained about the pain when he was first brought in!'

'Maybe he was too concussed.'

'Well I'm the one who feels concussed now. His father's threatening to sue the hospital for negligence and causing his son unnecessary pain. That's why they've hauled me in to discover whether there are grounds for negligence or not.'

'Oh, Damian!'

'There's more,' he added. 'Mr Mullins – that's the boy's father – fancies himself as a bit of a lawyer. He's also accusing me of giving the wrong dose of drugs to his son.'

'And do you think you did?'

'Not really.'

'Well then, he has no case against you.'

'But Mr Mullins thinks he has, Suzie. What's more, he's found a doctor to support him. So now I've got to answer two charges. Negligence and mistaken prescription. If the charges stick, I'm out of the hospital. Bella won't need to worry about Dr Damian Holt any more. I'll be back home in Australia, trying to find a job.'

Now he was sure of her help, Jamie set about winning Bella over completely. Even from his hospital bed, he could be charming. Bella loved his deep voice and easy manner. She found herself feeling drawn very close to him. It made her feel confident enough to ask him some more personal questions.

'What do you do, Jamie?' she said. 'Your job, I mean.'

'Oh – I'm a money man.'

'I knew it! I told Mark you were a banker.'

'That's right,' he said. 'An investment banker.'

'That sounds wonderful. I guessed you must have a high-flying job of some sort. I mean, you could never buy a house in Gallagher Road and a Mercedes on a nurse's salary.'

'That's true,' he smiled.

'Do you go abroad as well?'

'Yes, usually several times a year.'

'I'd love a job with a chance to travel.'

'Jumping on and off planes can get a bit boring.'

'I'd love it!' said Bella, her eyes shining.

Jamie smiled at her. 'Maybe I'll take you with me one day.'

'You really mean it?' she breathed.

'Why not? How about Paris?'

'Or Rome? Or Venice?' Bella was warming to the game.

'Take your pick,' he said, smoothly. 'I always pay my debts. Do me that big favour and you'll get your reward.'

'Thanks, Jamie!'

'As long as you tell nobody – *nobody* – about it.'

'It'll be our secret.'

'Just remember that, OK? Or the deal's off.'

'I'll remember,' Bella assured him.

Jamie lay back on his pillows and looked at her shrewdly.

'Now tell me all about yourself, Bella.'

'There's nothing much to tell,' she confessed.

'Where were you born and brought up? What made you want to be a nurse? Tell me how you like to relax. What you like to do. Come on – I want to know everything.'

Bella was flattered by his interest and she launched into an account of her life. She didn't get very far. She was still talking about her schooldays when the door opened and Sister Judd breezed in with a visitor. He was a big, brawny man in his thirties. His hair was close-cropped and he wore a smart charcoal-grey suit.

Sister Judd stopped dead in her tracks when she saw Bella.

'What are *you* doing in here, Nurse Denton?' she demanded. 'You have no need to be in this room.'

'Sorry, Sister,' muttered Bella.

'Go to my office at once. We need to talk about this.'

Bella turned hopefully to Jamie for support but he said nothing. He seemed quite taken aback by his unexpected visitor. Bella walked slowly towards the door. As she went out, she heard the man introducing himself to Jamie in a deep, formal voice.

'Good morning, Mr Stoddard. My name is Foxwell, Detective-Inspector Foxwell.'

Bella's heart started to thump.

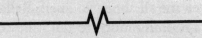

Karlene walked into the living room and gasped in alarm. Gordy was lying on his back in the middle of the floor. His face was flushed and he was panting heavily. Karlene rushed over to kneel beside him.

'Are you all right, Gordy?' she asked.

'No,' he gasped. 'I'm not.'

'What is it? You're sweating. Have you got a fever?'

'I've got everything.'

'I'll call a doctor.'

'No, Kar. Just get me a glass of water,' he groaned.

'When did this happen?'

'As soon as I got back,' he gulped. 'From that crazy, self-imposed torture. I went for a run.'

Karlene relaxed. So Gordy was not, after all, having a heart attack or some kind of seizure. In her eagerness to help him, she hadn't noticed his tracksuit top and black shorts. Gordy's legs were sturdy and white. They made her want to giggle.

'What's so funny?'

'Nothing,' she spluttered.

'Just get that water,' he gasped.

Karlene went into the kitchen and returned with a glass of cold water. She helped Gordy into a sitting position and held the glass to his lips. He drank the water in one go. She noticed his legs again and grinned once more.

'Don't laugh!' he protested. 'I feel like a corpse.'

'Sorry, Gordy. Let me help you up,' she gulped, trying to control her desire to laugh.

She helped him on to the sofa and sat beside him. His breathing was less laboured now and his cheeks looked less flushed. She tried not to look at his legs again.

'What made you go out running?' she said.

'It's all part of my fitness campaign,' said Gordy, lying back on the cushions.

'Oh yes – what's it in aid of, Gordy?'

'Me, of course,' he said. 'The newer, slimmer, fitter Dr Robbins. I've let myself go. Those canteen meals are so stodgy. From now on, I'll take regular exercise. Get myself in shape.'

'I'm all in favour of that. Why don't we start playing squash together again?'

'That's a good idea, Kar. That's a real fitness test.'

'Swimming would help you as well.'

'Don't worry. That's on my list, too. By the time I've finished, they won't be able to resist me.' Gordy lowered his voice. 'Don't tell the others, will you?' he whispered.

'Tell them what?'

'I'm going to tell you if you promise not to tell them. It's personal, Kar. I can trust you, but Bel would only make fun of me. And I'd hate to admit it to Suze.'

'Admit what?' Karlene was getting irritated.

'I'm pining!'

'Who for?'

'A girlfriend. Miss Right. Miss Wrong. Miss Anyone. I don't know what's happened to me, Kar. When I first came to med school, I could chat girls up with no problem. All of a sudden, my charms don't work any more. I haven't taken a girl out for weeks.'

'You took Suzie to that rock concert.'

'That was different. She didn't come as my... well, you know. My date. That's what I need. A date – a night out with a girlfriend. Someone who really fancies me.'

'*And* doesn't laugh at your legs!'

'Someone who'll *love* me,' he wailed. 'It's not much to ask, is it? I'm young and attractive. I've got a car – I've got a great collection of CDs. I've got a promising future ahead of me. I've got everything, Kar.'

'Except a girlfriend,' she added, trying to look sympathetic.

Gordy gritted his teeth with determination.

'She's out there somewhere. And I'll find her.'

Bella was waiting anxiously in Sister Judd's office. She'd been caught in the private unit and would really be told off now. What she feared most was being dismissed from her duties in Mendip Ward. It would separate her from Jamie and send her back into the clutches of Sister Killeen. She'd certainly tear strips off her for being thrown out of Mendip Ward. Bella shivered.

Sister Judd stormed in, shutting the door firmly behind her. She looked larger than ever as she loomed over her student nurse. Bella could see the anger in her eyes.

'Well?' she demanded.

'I'm sorry, Sister,' said Bella.

'I don't want an apology. I want an explanation.'

Bella cleared her throat and shifted her feet. 'I...I was worried about Ja...Mr Stoddard,' she stammered.

'It's not your place to be worried. He is a private patient and therefore nothing whatsoever to do with you.'

'I saw him being rushed off to surgery this morning, Sister Judd. He was in such agony. I wanted to check on him, that's all.'

'That's not all, is it?'

'Yes it is, Sister.'

'Don't lie to me, Bella. Or I'll send you straight back to Sister Killeen. Is that what you want?'

'No!' said Bella in alarm.

'Then tell me the truth.'

'That *is* the truth, Sister Judd. I was just concerned about a patient.'

'But that's only part of the truth, isn't it?'

The Sister waved her to a chair then went to sit behind her desk. Her eyes never left Bella, who was beginning to quail beneath her glare. Hands clasped together, Sister Judd leaned forward.

'Let's try again, shall we?' she said.

'If you like.'

'What were you doing in Mr Stoddard's room?'

'You could say I was being nosy,' admitted Bella.

'That's more like it.'

'But only because of Gordy and Suzie. Those friends of mine. They were actually there – at the scene of the explosion.'

'Yes, yes. I think you mentioned them before,' said the Sister.

'They asked me to find out how Mr Stoddard was.'

'You're here to work, Nurse Denton. Not to satisfy the inquiries of a couple of friends.'

'But they feel *involved*,' argued Bella. 'And it's not just ghoulish curiosity, they're both based here, at the hospital. Gordy's at medical school and Suzie's training to be a radiodog...er, I mean, a radiographer. So their interest was professional, as well, Sister.'

The senior nurse was slightly mollified by that but she didn't let Bella off the hook. She waved a finger at Bella to make her point.

'Keep away from Mr Stoddard,' she warned.

'Yes, Sister Judd.'

'He needs complete rest and he insists on his privacy.'

'Yes, Sister, I know.'

'The last thing he wants is you barging in there. Stay away. Otherwise... ' Her voice became more threatening. 'Otherwise, I will send you straight back to Sister Killeen with a poor report.'

'Please, don't do that, Sister,' pleaded Bella. 'I like it here.'

'Then stick to the rules.'

'I will, Sister, I promise. No more unauthorised visits.'

'No more curiosity about Mr Stoddard. Is that clear?'

'Very clear, Sister Judd.'

Bella felt a surge of relief. She had survived. When the Sister waved a hand dismissively, Bella moved towards the door and opened it. But something else jogged her memory.

'What did that detective want with him, Sister?' she asked.

Sister Judd began to smoulder. Bella turned away quickly. She might have pushed her luck too far this time.

───────\\/\\───────

'I was so annoyed with myself,' said Karlene. 'Just when I seemed to be getting through to Daisy, I went and said the wrong thing.'

'You touched a raw spot,' observed Mark.

'I know. One minute I was her friend and now she treats me like her worst enemy.'

'You'll win her round, Kar,' said Gordy. 'She wouldn't have turned to you in the first place if she didn't like you.'

Karlene nodded. 'That's what Catherine White said. With all her years of experience, she couldn't get a peep out of Daisy, but somehow I managed to find the key.'

'And you'll do it again,' Gordy assured her.

'I really hope so.'

The three friends were seated at their table in the kitchen. Irritated by the way Karlene laughed at his legs, Gordy had changed out of his running gear. Now he was wearing a pair of jeans and one of the gaudy shirts which had given him his nickname. Mark had come home hungry and was munching a toasted sandwich.

'It's such a vital part of the job,' he remarked.

'What is?' said Karlene.

'Psychology.'

'I certainly found that out with Daisy.'

'It isn't enough to try and heal the physical symptoms. You have to be able to work out how a patient's mind works.'

'That's why I'll be such a great doctor,' said Gordy, airily. 'When it comes to psychology, I've got the touch. I can read people's minds easily.'

'Then prove it,' said Mark, passing his cup across the table. 'Read mine.'

Gordy picked up the teapot and filled his cup for him.

'Something's stopping Daisy from communicating with anyone,' said Karlene.

'Let *me* speak to her,' said Gordy, getting into his stride.

'You'd only frighten her off. Especially if you were wearing a pair of shorts!'

Gordy looked hurt. 'Some women think I've got nice legs!'

'Yes – nice and funny,' said Karlene, smiling.

'What you must do,' said Mark, seriously, 'is to get a more detailed profile of Daisy. Talk to her parents and her schoolfriends. They might be able to give you the pieces of the jigsaw that are missing.'

'That's a great idea,' said Karlene.

'Daisy obviously wants to talk to someone or she wouldn't have let you chat to her at all. But she's confused right now.'

'She certainly doesn't want to talk about her accident.'

'If that's what it was,' noted Mark.

'You mean, someone may have *pushed* her off that bus?'

'I don't know, Karlene, but I think you should find out more about it all before you try and speak to her. You don't want to upset her again.'

'I'd hate to do that.'

'What was the name Daisy mentioned?'

'Miss Whitlow – she teaches games at Daisy's school.'

'Why not contact her? Perhaps she can help.'

'Marco's firing on all cylinders today,' said Gordy.

'I'm glad somebody is,' teased Karlene.

'I could have told you exactly the same as Marco.'

'But you didn't, did you, Gordy? You just got all pompous and self-important about being a great doctor.'

'Well I am,' he said. 'Or at least, I will be.'

'A great doctor with funny legs?'

'Stop going on about them, Kar!'

Mark finished his sandwich and looked at his watch.

'Bella's late. I wonder what's keeping her.'

'Maybe she's found a new boyfriend,' suggested Gordy.

'I don't think so. The only man she's interested in at the moment is Jamie Stoddard. Bella's getting very keen on him. If she's not careful, it'll land her in serious trouble.'

'You know Bel,' said Gordy. 'She thrives on danger.'

'Sister Killeen will skin her alive if Bella lets her down. We were sent over to Mendip Ward to make a positive contribution. Sister Killeen keeps telling us that every student nurse is an advertisement for her. If we foul up, it reflects badly on our tutor.'

'Sounds reasonable,' said Karlene. 'But Bella's not the only one who's late. Where's Suzie? She should have been back ages ago.'

'She came in and went out again,' explained Gordy.

'Where's she gone?'

'Just out, Kar. For a drink, that's all.'

'Who with?'

'A friend.'

'Male or female?'

'I have no idea,' he said, tactfully. 'I never pry into other people's lives. All I know is, Suzie popped out for an hour to meet a friend in the pub.'

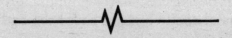

Damian drained his glass and rose from the table. He was feeling much better now. As he and Suzie went out through the exit, he put his hand on her arm.

'Thanks, Suzie.'

'All I did was listen.'

'That's exactly what I needed. A sympathetic ear. I hoped Bella would provide it, but she couldn't.'

'Did you try to talk to her?'

'She didn't give me much chance.'

'Well, don't be too hard on her, Damian. She has her faults, but Bella's very kind-hearted. If she knew you were having problems, I'm sure she'd try and help.'

'It's too late for that now. I don't need Bella – I've got you.' He smiled warmly at her. 'Come on. I'll walk you back.'

'OK, thanks.'

As they strolled side by side, Suzie was glad she had spent an hour in the pub with Damian. She saw a new side to him. Before, she'd always thought of him as a guy who loved to party. Now she realized that he was also a serious young doctor with a real commitment to his work. It was a way of life to him.

'I love being at the hospital,' he said.

'In spite of what happened?'

'Everyone makes mistakes under pressure. I just hope I won't be punished for the one I made.

In spite of all its stresses and strains, I get a real buzz out of working in Casualty. It's right at the cutting edge of medicine.'

'I'm sure you've got nothing to worry about, Damian.'

'I hope not.'

'The hospital managers aren't stupid. They know a good doctor when they see one. I'm sure they'll make allowances for one small error.'

'*Two* errors, Suzie. Failing to spot rib damage on that boy and prescribing the wrong dose of drugs.'

'Who says it *was* the wrong dose?'

'This doctor who Mr Mullins has produced.'

'And what do your colleagues say?'

'They'd have given the identical dose.'

'There you are, then,' she said. 'Call them as witnesses in your defence. Fight this Mr Mullins. Clear your name.'

'I intend to, Suzie.'

An ambulance raced past on its way to the hospital. Damian gave a wry smile. If he was on duty, he would be handling the new emergency. There was an excitement in working in Casualty that he would hate to lose.

They chatted happily all the way back to Suzie's house. Damian began to thank her all over again and Suzie held up her hand.

'I was just pleased to help,' she said. 'If you need me again, any time, just shout. And I promise to say nothing to Bella.'

'She'd go mad.'

'Then we'll keep the whole thing secret.'

'Thanks, Suzie. I knew I could count on you.'

Damian gave her an affectionate kiss on the cheek.

'You double-crossing rat!' yelled a voice behind them.

They turned to see Bella stalking down the path towards them.

'You didn't waste much time, did you, Suzie?' she snapped. 'As soon as my back's turned, you take my boyfriend.'

'That's not what I'm doing, Bella,' cried Suzie.

'No!' added Damian. 'Anyway, I'm not your boyfriend, remember? You broke it off!'

Bella was fuming. 'All I remember is the things you said to me, Dr Damian Holt. That I was the most dynamic girl you'd ever met; that I made all the others look insignificant. I daresay you've been saying the same to Suzie right now.'

'No, Bella, he hasn't,' said Suzie.

'You're mistaken, Bella – things are not the way they look,' insisted Damian.

'Pull the other one!' Bella snorted.

'We had a drink together, that's all,' he explained. 'There's no harm in that, is there? Suzie and I are just friends.'

'I can see that!'

'Calm down, Bella,' urged Suzie.

'How would you like it if I snitched *your* boyfriend?'

'It's nothing like that – honestly!'

'I can vouch for that,' said Damian. 'In fact–'

'Don't lie to me,' interrupted Bella, brushing past them to unlock the front door. 'Every picture tells a story. And this one is pretty sordid. I'm not surprised at Damian. I'd expect it from him. But I thought better of you, Suzie. I never imagined you'd do anything like this!'

'I wouldn't – and I didn't!'

'You're being really unfair – to both of us,' said Damian.

'Oh, shut up!' shouted Bella. 'Goodnight and good riddance!'

Once again, Damian had the door slammed in his face.

— CHAPTER EIGHT —

Karlene forked the last of her scrambled egg into her mouth and washed it down with some coffee. Mark was deep in the morning paper. She cleared the breakfast things and put them in a bowl of water to soak.

'Your turn to do the washing-up today, Mark.'

'What?' He looked up. 'Oh, yes. Just leave it, Karlene.'

'Have you got a busy day today?'

'We're working in Mendip Ward again. It's good fun, though.'

'Don't you mind being the dogsbody?'

'It's all good experience, Karlene.' Mark put his newspaper aside. 'Talking of that, I was fascinated by that little snippet Bella gave us last night – about Jamie Stoddard.'

'About him having a visit from the police, you mean?'

'Yes, I'd love to know what that was all about.'

'Bella didn't stick around long enough to guess,' said Karlene. 'She raced off to her room the moment Suzie came in. *That's* the mystery I want explained.'

'Suzie said it was all a misunderstanding.'

'I hope so. We don't want any problems in the house.'

Karlene began to search through her handbag

to make sure she had everything she needed. Mark cleared away his plate and coffee mug.

'Will you be seeing Daisy again?'

'Seeing her, yes,' she said. 'Talking to her, probably not.'

'She may feel more communicative today.'

'No, Mark. I'm afraid she'll try and avoid me from now on. It's such a shame – I'm sure she desperately needs a friend.'

Suzie came downstairs and into the kitchen.

'Morning, guys. Is Bella not up yet?' she asked.

'Up and gone,' said Karlene. 'She was leaving the house as I came down for breakfast.'

'That's a bit unusual for her,' said Mark. 'Bella likes to drag it out until the last possible moment. Why did she want to get to the hospital so early?'

'She didn't,' decided Suzie. 'She was avoiding me. I was hoping to make peace with her this morning, but it looks as if the battle's still on.'

'Have you two fallen out?' asked Karlene.

'I haven't – but Bella has.'

'Why? Whatever for?'

Suzie sighed. 'It's over Damian.'

'Damian Holt?'

'I had a drink with him last night. But that's *all* I had. It wasn't a date. Far from it. Damian simply wanted to discuss something with me.'

'And Bella found out about it, I suppose?'

'She saw us saying good night, Karlene. Bella walked up at the very moment Damian was giving me a kiss on the cheek.'

'*Now* I understand!'

'But she and Damian have split up,' said Mark.

Suzie smiled. 'That doesn't seem to make any difference to Bella.'

'She's a real dog-in-the-manger,' said Karlene. '*She* doesn't want Damian to be her boyfriend but she resents anyone else going out with him.'

'I thought she might have calmed down by this morning, but obviously she hasn't. It's ridiculous. I don't fancy Damian. He's just not my type.'

'But you did have a drink with him,' reminded Mark.

'Yes, I did.'

'In secret.'

'We didn't want Bella to know about it.'

'I can see why.'

'We knew she'd go off the deep end.' Suzie shook her head sadly. 'If there was anything between me and Damian, I'd have more sense than to bring him back here so Bella could see him kissing me on the doorstep.'

Karlene grinned. 'I thought he only kissed you on the cheek, Suzie.'

They all laughed and it seemed to break the tension. Suzie was pleased that Karlene and Mark believed her version of the evening. And she was grateful that they didn't ask her what she and Damian had been discussing. Their conversation had been in strictest confidence and she had promised not to tell anybody about it.

Suzie filled the electric kettle for herself and plugged it in.

'Where's Gordy?' she asked.

'You've missed him as well,' said Mark.

'Don't tell me *he* left early! Not Gordy.'

'He was out of the starting blocks at seven-thirty. He's trying to get fit,' explained Mark. 'Gordy has decided he'll run to work from now on.'

'In a pair of shorts,' added Karlene, laughing. 'Those legs of his will certainly stop the traffic.'

'Why the sudden urge to get fit?' asked Suzie.

Karlene smiled. 'It's part of his search for love,' she said.

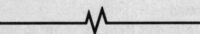

Gordy was panting heavily by the time he reached the garden at the back of the hospital. With his hands on his knees, he paused to catch his breath. He was wearing just a singlet and running shorts. His clothes were in a rucksack on his back. It wasn't a long run from the house but it had exhausted him and he needed several minutes to recover.

He was still bent double when the girl bumped into him.

'Oops!' she said. 'I'm sorry. I didn't see you there.'

'Don't worry. Can I help you?' he asked, straightening up.

'My name's Jessica. Jessica Roe. I'm visiting my boyfriend.'

'In the hospital garden?' asked Gordy, grinning at her.

'No, no,' said Jessica. 'He's in Carlton Ward. I was just trying to find my way there.'

'Then you'll have to go round to the main entrance. But you'll have a long wait. Visitors aren't allowed in for a couple of hours yet. You're much too early.'

'Oh, I see.'

Jessica flashed him a brief smile and Gordy saw what an attractive girl she was. Short and shapely, she had beautiful green eyes set in an oval face. There was an energy about her that reminded him of Bella. She was wearing a fitted T-shirt and a satin skirt.

'Are you Security?' she asked.

'No, no. I'm a medical student.'

She was impressed. 'You're going to be a doctor!'

'Eventually.'

'You must be clever, then.'

'I have my moments,' said Gordy, nonchalantly. When he looked at Jessica more closely, he felt a pang of envy.

Jessica's boyfriend was very lucky. She seemed to read his thoughts.

'Kish is only in here for a few days. My boyfriend – he's having a minor operation.'

'He'll be thrilled to see you, Jessica.'

'I hope so. I really want to cheer him up.'

'You'll do that without even trying!'

She smiled at the compliment then looked around properly for the first time.

'Well, I'll be on my way...sorry, what's your name?

'Robbins,' he said. 'Gordy Robbins.'

'Thanks for your help, Gordy.'

'Any time.'

She gave him her biggest smile before heading off towards the front entrance. Gordy went in the opposite direction but something made him turn round when he reached the corner of the building. Jessica Roe had doubled back. Instead of going to the front entrance, she was scanning the fire escape at the back of the building.

Gordy was utterly baffled.

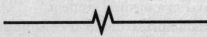

'It's nothing to do with you, Mark,' said Bella.

'Well I think it is.'

'No, this is between me and Suzie. And that rat, Damian.'

'He's not a rat, Bella.'

'I *saw* them together.'

'And overreacted?' suggested Mark.

'I was a model of self-control, believe me. What I really wanted to do was bang their heads together.'

'What would you have gained by doing that?'

'A great deal of satisfaction!' said Bella, emphatically.

Mark sighed heavily as he tried to reason with her.

'Bella,' he said.' Five of us share that house. It's not the ideal arrangement, but it does work, if we try hard enough. We all have to pull together.'

'The way Suzie and Damian were doing?' she said, angrily.

'No! Forget Damian. He's not part of this equation. You and Suzie are. That's why you've got to talk to her.'

'Stop taking her side.'

'I'm not taking anybody's side. All I'm asking you to do is hear Suzie out. For the sake of all of us. What do you think it's like for me, Karlene and Gordy, when you two are at each other's throats?'

Bella nodded. She could see his point. At the same time, she was still very angry with Suzie. She thought she'd been betrayed by one of her closest friends, and it was a really nasty feeling.

'Will you at least speak to her?' asked Mark.

'I'll think about it.'

'You can't go on ignoring her, Bella.'

She looked defiant. But before Mark could say anything more, Sister Judd came into the laundry room to separate them. While Mark was asked to bring clean bed linen to the ward, Bella was told to help with serving lunch to the patients. It was over an hour before they even got close enough for a brief word.

The whole day, Bella was wondering how Jamie was getting on, but she had no means of finding out. Sister Judd was watching her every minute – at least that's what it felt like – and she didn't dare approach the private unit again. She resigned herself to not seeing him.

At the end of the afternoon, she got a surprise. She was just refilling a patient's water jug, when she happened to glance down the ward. A hand emerged from the last cubicle at the far end and an index finger seemed to beckon to her to come over.

Making sure she wasn't seen, Bella slipped across to the cubicle and darted in through the open door. She was astonished to see Jamie standing there. He was wearing pyjamas and had a dressing gown draped over his shoulders.

'Jamie!' she exclaimed.

'Shh! You must keep your voice down,' he whispered.

'What are you doing in here?'

'Hoping to see you. I knew you wouldn't be able to reach me, so I decided to try to get to you.'

'You shouldn't have,' she said with concern. 'You're not well enough to get out of bed. Look what happened the last time.'

'I feel much better now, Bella. And I've been much more careful moving about this time.' He grinned. 'Aren't you pleased to see me?'

'Of course I am!'

'Good. When I peered round my door earlier on, I saw someone taking the bed linen away from this cubicle. So I guessed that it was empty.'

'Sister Judd will kill us if she finds us in here,' said Bella, looking over her shoulder. 'She came down on me like a ton of bricks yesterday.'

'That was my fault – sorry.'

'You weren't to blame.'

'Of course I was. I invited you into my room.'

'It was fun being with you, Jamie. But I must admit I was surprised when that policeman turned up. What did he want?'

'He's a Detective-Inspector – Ron Foxwell. It was just a routine visit,' he said, calmly. 'He just wanted to update me on the damage to my house. They've had a couple of fire inspectors in there. Ron Foxwell brought me their report.'

'And *was* it a gas explosion?'

'Well – sort of.'

'So you'll be able to sue the gas board?'

'Probably. Not that there's any need. The house is insured – they'll pay for all the damage.'

'To the building, maybe,' she argued, 'but what about the damage to you? And the inconvenience of being thrown out of your own home. Will the insurance cover the cost of a hotel or some other accommodation?'

'Leave that to me, Bella. All I wanted to do was explain why I'd had a visit from the law. It must have been a shock when you realized it was the Bill.'

'It was.'

'Well, he's gone now.'

'I'm relieved to hear that, Jamie.' She looked guiltily towards the door again. 'Look, I can't stay any longer.'

'One more thing, Bella.'

'Yes?'

'Remember when I asked if you'd do me a big favour? Are you still on for that?'

'Of course I am.' She looked serious.

'Because I may need to ask you any minute.'

'I'll be glad to help, Jamie.'

He smiled. 'I knew you would, Bella. And when I'm out of here, I'll take you off to Paris to celebrate. Is it a deal?'

He winked at her and her legs turned to jelly.

CHAPTER NINE

Catherine White had arranged the meeting for her. When Karlene had expressed an interest in speaking to Daisy's mother, she had contacted Vera Collier at once. Now, Karlene was meeting her in the waiting room that afternoon.

'Hello, Mrs Collier,' she said.

'How do you do?'

'It's very nice of you to come in and see me.'

'I was coming in, anyway. To bring Daisy.'

'Of course.'

Vera Collier was a short, stocky woman in her late thirties. Her attractive features were distorted with anxiety and her long hair was unkempt. Even though she was wearing her best suit, she still looked untidy. Her voice was breathy and there was a harassed look about her.

'I'm so sorry about Daisy's accident.'

'We all are, Miss—'

'Call me Karlene, please. She's such a bright girl.'

'She was. But the spark seems to have gone out of her.'

'Does she talk much – to you and your husband?'

'My husband and I are separated,' said Mrs Collier, bitterly. 'Daisy and I live alone together. And – no. She doesn't say very much at home.'

'What was she like before her accident?'

'She talked all the time – morning, noon and night.'

'So her silence is only since the accident?'

'She's just being stubborn,' said Daisy's mother.

Karlene tried to figure it out. Bringing up a child wasn't easy at the best of times. But when a wife was separated from her husband, and trying to look after a disabled daughter, the burden would be very heavy. Vera Collier seemed to be wilting beneath the weight of it already.

'I had a chat with Daisy,' said Karlene.

'Mrs White told me – that you'd actually managed to get through to her.'

'Only a little bit, I'm afraid. As soon as I asked her about the accident itself, she refused to speak to me.'

Mrs Collier looked down. 'Yes, she would.'

'Why, do you think?'

'Because she always does.'

'You know I'm trying to *help* your daughter, Mrs Collier.'

'I know, and I do appreciate it.'

'Daisy's such an interesting girl with so much going for her in spite of everything that's happened.'

'She can't see it that way yet.'

'That's why we have to convince her. We must try and instil some confidence in her, make her see she can still lead an active and fulfilled life.'

'I've tried,' said Vera Collier, wearily. 'But she doesn't listen.'

'There has to be a reason for that.'

'There is – like I say, Daisy's stubborn.'

'It's more than stubborness, though, isn't it?'

'I know my daughter,' said Mrs Collier, defensively.

'I'm sure you do.'

Karlene changed the subject slightly and began chatting in more general terms about the work of the physiotherapists at the hospital. Then slowly she started to come back to the most important question.

'Were you on the bus when the accident happened, Mrs Collier?'

There was a long pause. 'Yes,' she said, hardly audible.

'So you saw everything?'

'Yes, I did.'

'It must have been dreadful for you. Can you bear to...tell me about it?'

There was a longer pause. Vera Collier ran a hand through her straggly hair and took a handkerchief out to blow her nose. When she finally spoke, it was in a whisper.

'Not being able to help,' she said. 'That was the worst thing. Seeing Daisy hit by that van and not being able to *do* anything for her. It was horrifying!'

'Where did it happen?'

'In the middle of the main street.'

'At the bus stop?' asked Karlene, gently.

'About a quarter of a mile away.'

'So the bus wasn't slowing down for the stop?'

'No, it was moving quite fast.'

'What made Daisy jump off? Surely she knew how dangerous that was?'

'Ask her,' whispered Mrs Collier. 'She won't talk about it because it was all her own fault, that's why.'

'Her own fault?'

'She did it on purpose,' said Daisy's mother, suddenly angry. 'Just to spite me.'

But Mrs Collier's anger turned to remorse at once and she burst into floods of tears. Karlene put a comforting arm around her, as she dabbed at her eyes with a handkerchief. She made a huge effort to pull herself together.

'I'm sorry,' said Karlene. 'I shouldn't have asked.'

Vera Collier stared ahead of her through unseeing, watery eyes. 'We'd had a terrible argument,' she murmured.

'What about?' Karlene leaned closer to her.

'It's silly, I can't even remember now. We had so many rows. Daisy was always arguing with me. It got worse when my husband left. He knew how to deal with her – I don't.' She held

Karlene's arm. 'I don't want you to think I don't love my daughter, because I do. I adore Daisy. She's all I've got. But she always goes a bit too far.'

'Is that what she did on the bus?'

'She answered me back very rudely.'

'And an argument developed?'

'I started to yell at her,' said Vera Collier, shakily.

'What did Daisy do?'

'She yelled back. She told me she hated me.'

'All children say that at some time, Mrs Collier.'

'But she meant it,' said Vera Collier, hurt by the memory. 'At least at the time she did. She proved that. She said she'd do anything just to get away from me. And then...'

'She jumped?'

Vera Collier was crying again now.

'I think she just wanted to frighten me. It was an impulsive, stupid thing to do. I'm sure it never entered her head that she might be seriously hurt. But a lorry swerved in close to the bus and...'

Words failed her as she relived the memory, though Karlene did her best to comfort her. Later she felt that her talk with Daisy's mother was a painful experience, but it had revealed something new about Daisy. Now, Karlene felt, she really might be able to help the young girl.

As Bella was leaving the hospital that evening, she saw him crossing the car park. Damian was looking rather dejected. There was none of the customary spring in his step. He looked up and saw Bella and, with a tired smile, begain to pick his way towards her through the cars. But Bella didn't wait for him. Ignoring Damian completely, she headed for the exit and was soon lost amongst the crowd in the main street.

She was still angry about what she saw as a betrayal but she had something to console her now. Damian might be out of her life but he'd been replaced by somebody much more exciting. Jamie Stoddard.

'Paris!' she said to herself. 'I fancy a trip to Paris!'

Bella never paused to ask herself what Jamie might want her to do in exchange. And she didn't stop to wonder why he had singled her out especially. Bella was used to men taking an interest in her, so she took it for granted. Jamie was just the latest in a long line of guys who had fallen for her.

'Only this time – I hit the jackpot!'

As a bus came round the bend towards her she saw the name on the front of it. Gallagher Road. Bella acted on impulse. Turning round, she ran back to the stop and flagged the bus down. It was soon carrying her to the road where Jamie lived.

She wanted to know as much as possible about him, and his house was the ideal starting-place. When the bus had dropped her off, she could see what an exclusive area it was. All the properties were detached, with big gardens at the front and back. It was a stark contrast to the mean little street where she and her friends lived.

Jamie's house was easy to pick out. It was supported by scaffolding and covered in tarpaulins. His Mercedes had been towed away and the garage was no more than a pile of rubble. Yellow and black tape surrounded the entire property and a policeman was standing outside, moving on some inquisitive children.

Bella paused outside the house. One of the tarpaulins hung down over what had been a bay window and the wind was making it flap. As it did so, she caught a glimpse of two men on their hands and knees, sifting their way through the wrecked interior.

'What are they doing?' she asked boldly, as she approached the policeman.

'Just move along, miss,' he said, politely.

'But there are two men inside my friend's house. You see, I know Jamie Stoddard. We're very close?'

'He's the owner, isn't he?'

'That's right. I met him at the hospital, I'm a student nurse there.'

'He's lucky to be alive, that young man.'

'He must be,' said Bella, surveying the debris, 'to get out of this in one piece. I've told him to sue the gas board.'

'Oh, why?' said the policeman, raising an eyebrow.

'Because they were responsible for the explosion.'

'Oh yes? Who told you that, young lady?'

'Jamie did. Detective-Inspector Foxwell came to the hospital with a report. I saw him myself. There was a build up of gas and then – boom!'

'That's not quite how it happened, I'm afraid.'

'Jamie should know, he was *there*.'

'Probably didn't know what hit him. Actually, it was a lethal device – or so our bomb expert reckons.'

'*Bomb* expert?'

'Yes,' said the policeman. 'That's why the lads are going through the place for clues. It's nothing to do with the gas board, the damage was caused by an explosive device.'

Bella was shocked. She couldn't take in the implications of what she was hearing. She felt the colour drain from her face.

'Sorry...What are you saying?' she gulped.

'Your friend isn't in hospital because of an accident.'

'What happened, then?'

'Someone tried to kill him.'

———————————/\/———————————

'When was this, Damian?' asked Suzie.

'About twenty minutes ago,' he said.

'Did she see you?'

'I'm certain she did. But as soon as I walked towards her, she headed for the exit.'

'That means she's still mad at us.'

'At *me*, you mean,' said Damian.

'But I have to live with her, remember. She's a friend.'

He'd been waiting for Suzie to come out of the hospital and persuaded her to have coffee with him in a nearby snack bar. Suzie could see that he was upset and she put it down to his encounter with Bella.

'What were you going to say to her?' she asked.

'Oh, I don't know,' said Damian, dejectedly.

'Would you have said sorry to her?'

'Maybe. I hadn't really thought it out.'

'But she didn't stay around to listen.'

'No,' he said with a wan smile. 'But at least she couldn't slam a door in my face this time.'

'Leave it to me. I'll handle Bella.'

'You'd better wear a pair of asbestos gloves, then.'

Suzie grinned. 'I might just do that.'

'But whatever you do, don't tell her everything.'

'I won't, Damian. You can trust me.'

'It's embarrassing enough for me, as it is. I don't want it to go any further. Especially not to Bella's ears.'

'I'm sure she'd be sympathetic.'

'No she wouldn't, Suzie. She'd be even madder.'

'Why?'

'Because I confided in you. All right, I *tried* to tell her, but that won't count – Bella can be very jealous sometimes, as we've both found out. Don't give her any more excuses.'

'Don't worry, I won't.'

'Thanks, Suzie.'

'Anyhow, there's no reason why she should ever know about it.'

'Unless I get kicked out of the hospital. Everybody will know then. DOCTOR SACKED FOR NEGLIGENCE. They'll probably put my picture in the paper.'

'Stop fearing the worst,' she said. 'The Board of Inquiry won't rush to dismiss a good doctor. It's bad publicity. And the charges levelled against you still have to be proved.'

'That's true.'

'If you put up a strong defence, they're bound to be impressed and that will make them want to keep you.'

'I'm not so sure about that, Suzie.'

'You didn't really do anything grossly negligent.'

'The hospital thinks so.'

'What do you mean?'

'They don't want to delay a decision any longer. The Board of Inquiry has been brought forward to next week.'

'That's great news, Damian!'

'Is it?'

'Yes, you won't have to sweat it out any longer. The whole matter can be cleared up and you can carry on with your job in the normal way.'

'That's what I wanted to tell you, Suzie,' he said. 'I haven't got a job at the moment.'

'What? You're not in Casualty any more?'

'No.' Damian looked like a broken man. 'They think that the negligence charge is a serious one. I've been suspended from the hospital until the inquiry's over.'

Gordy had left the Medical School and taken a short cut through the garden behind the main hospital block. But he didn't get very far. As his gaze turned towards the back of the building, he saw a small figure clinging to the fire escape. She was trying to stretch out her leg to a windowsill on the first floor. Gordy stared in amazement. Someone was trying to climb into the hospital.

He ran over to the fire escape and looked up.

'Hey!' he yelled. 'What d'you think you're doing!'

But his shout made the intruder panic. Her hand lost its grip on the metal staircase and her foot lost its purchase on the windowsill. To his horror, Gordy saw the figure falling through the air towards him. Before he could move, he was knocked flat by a shapely body. They both rolled, winded, on to the grass.

'Aouw!' complained Gordy.

'You frightened me!' she said.

'You didn't have to land on top of me!' Gordy gasped.

As he untangled himself he recognized the girl. It was Jessica Roe. Now she was wearing a shirt, jeans and trainers and her hair was hidden under a baseball cap. A huge smile of relief spread across her face.

'It's *you*,' she said. 'Gordy – the doctor.'

'I'm more likely to finish up as a patient if you jump on me like that,' he said, pulling himself to his feet.

'You broke my fall, thank you.'

'What on earth were you doing you there? Are you crazy?'

'Looking in through that window,' she said, getting up and dusting herself off. 'Thank goodness I didn't have all that far to fall.'

'You shouldn't have been up there in the first place.'

'I know,' she admitted, 'but you won't tell anyone, will you?'

'I ought to.'

'Look, can we be friends?'

'Well...'

'Good.' She grinned, delighted. 'I liked you the moment I saw you, Gordy.'

'Did you? Oh, well, thank you, er...'

'Jessica,' she prompted.

'I remember. Jessica. Jessica Roe.'

'You might say I've fallen for you in a big way.'

They both laughed but Gordy wasn't going to be deflected. He couldn't let her climb about trying to get into the hospital – it was against the law.

'Really, I should report you to Security.'

'Please don't do that!' she begged.

'Then tell me what you were doing up there.'

'Trying to get in, and that window was open.'

'So are the main doors. Why not just walk in?'

'Because then they'd see me,' she wailed.

'Who would?'

'His family.'

'You're not making much sense, Jessica. Come here.'

He led her across to a bench and they sat down. They were both slightly shaken by the collision but they weren't hurt. Gordy noticed Jessica's perfume. It was enchanting. Her green eyes sparkled as she talked to him and he found it impossible not to like her.

'Now,' he insisted. 'I want the truth.'

'Promise you won't turn me in to Security?'

'Just tell me the story, first.'

'I want to see Kish, my boyfriend. We're crazy about each other,' she said. 'He's lying up there in bed, desperate to see me, and I can't get to him – they won't let me.'

'Who are "they"?'

'Kish's family. Kish is Bangladeshi and I'm not,' she explained with a sigh. 'They want him to marry a Bangladeshi girl – so they're trying to break us up.'

'They can't stop you visiting him, surely?'

'Yes they can. His elder brother's on guard in Reception – as soon as I went in through the front door, he came over and barred my way.'

'What does Kish say about all this?'

'He hates it as much as I do. Only there's not much he can do when he's lying in bed. No matter what it takes, I must get in to see Kish.'

'Even if it means climbing in through a window?'

'Even if it means digging a tunnel under the hospital,' she added, defiantly.

Gordy had to admire her determination. At the same time, he couldn't really encourage her to sneak into the building illegally. And she could have killed herself – this time she'd made a soft landing – next time she might not be so lucky.

'Do you see my problem, Gordy?' she asked.

'Yes,' he said, slowly, 'but there has to be another way round it.'

She grabbed his hand and stared earnestly into his face.

'What is it?' she said. 'I'd be so grateful if you could help. Tell me, Gordy. What would *you* do in my position?'

Bella was still shaking when she got back to the house. Mark had to calm her down before she could even begin to tell him what she'd discovered in Gallagher Road. They sat on the sofa in the living room.

'Are you sure about this, Bella?' he asked.

'Yes,' she said. 'The policeman told me.'

'The house was blown up – deliberately?'

'Someone tried to murder Jamie!'

'But why?'

'That's what I keep asking myself, Mark. I mean, he's the nicest person in the world. I'm sure Jamie wouldn't hurt a fly. Who could possibly want to kill him?'

'I don't know. But it does explain one thing.'

'What's that?'

'Why he's so obsessive about his privacy.'

'I don't understand,' said Bella.

'Well, he's paying for a room of his own because it gives him added security. In case the same people try again.'

She sat up suddenly, alarmed. 'Do you think they might?'

'Jamie obviously does,' said Mark. 'I bet that's why he tried to discharge himself from hospital. As long as he's in there, he's a sitting target.'

'It's awful!' cried Bella.

'I'm more concerned about you, you're the person he's befriended,' said Mark, looking worried.

'Well he likes me.'

'I'm sure he does, but he might also be putting you in danger. You don't want to be in the way if they come after him again. I should steer well clear of Jamie Stoddard if I were you.'

'But Mark, I'm his friend and I want to help him – protect him.'

'Bella!'

'I do. What sort of friend would I be if I walked out on him now? He needs me.'

'Maybe, but you don't need him.'

'I'm beginning to – we're quite close, Jamie has confided in me.'

'Then why didn't he mention the small matter of the bomb?' said Mark. 'He only tells you what he wants you to know, Bella. I had a feeling there was something odd about him. He's bad news. Forget him.'

'I don't want to.'

'You must,' pleaded Mark. 'For your own safety, Bella.'

'I keep telling you – he's a friend. Jamie's a really nice person.'

'He's also a marked man – a target for killers.'

'We don't *know* that.'

'Of course we do,' he argued. 'This wasn't a random attack on him, Bella, they planned it. They made a bomb, hid it in his house and detonated it when they knew he'd be inside. Those are the sort of people he's up against.'

'Then he needs all the help he can get.'

'From the police – but not from you!'

Bella hesitated; was still shocked by what she'd learned about the explosion but she refused to blame Jamie for not telling her the truth about it.

'He was trying to protect me,' she decided. 'From being hurt. That's why he said nothing about a bomb. He didn't want to frighten me. He's so considerate like that. I'm certain that's the explanation.'

'And I'm certain it's not!'

'You don't know him like I do, Mark.'

'I don't want to know him, Bella.'

'Well, I do.'

'Even if it makes you a target as well?'

'There's no chance of that,' she said. 'In any case, we don't even know if anyone's still out to get him. The police must be looking for them and they're probably miles away by now.'

'Don't count on it.'

Bella got up from the sofa and went into the kitchen to pour herself a glass of orange juice. Mark followed her.

'I'd hate anything to happen to you, Bella,' he said.

'It won't, Mark, don't worry.'

'Don't take any risks. Think of yourself.'

Bella sipped her orange juice as she tried to work out a way of speaking to her new friend. It was a problem but she was determined to solve it – somehow.

'I'll ask him to tell me the full story,' she said. 'I know he will. Jamie trusts me. If he really is a target, he can hide behind me. I'm not afraid,' she added boldly.

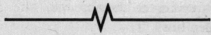

Her talk with Daisy's mother had been a revelation. Karlene thought she knew now why the young girl wouldn't talk about the accident which had led to the amputation of her leg. Unfortunately, she hadn't yet had an opportunity to spend any time with Daisy that afternoon. As soon as she'd completed her exercise programme, Daisy had wheeled herself out of the room – Karlene would just have to be patient.

In the meantime, she had thought of someone who might be able to help her. She found him in the gymnasium, working out with weights.

'Hi, Tony,' she said.

'Karlene!'

'How are you getting on?'

'Great!' He looked really pleased to see her.

Tony put the two dumbbells aside and grinned. He was a short, stocky young man with a crew cut. His face was pleasantly ugly. He wore a sleeveless vest and perspiration was streaming down his face and his chest. The lower half of his body had been paralysed in an accident during a rugby game. Now confined to a wheelchair, he was keen to develop his upper body strength and was a regular visitor to the hospital gym.

'Long time no see,' he observed.

'I've been busy.'

'Just finished work?'

'Yes, it's been a long day, Tony.'

'If you want to be a physio, you have to put up with the slog.'

'I know,' said Karlene. 'And the job has a lot of compensations – meeting people like you, for instance!'

Tony laughed. 'I've never been called a compensation before. I'm flattered.'

He reached for a towel and began to wipe the sweat off.

'I wanted to ask you a favour, Tony,' she said.

'Ask away.'

'I'm having a problem with a young patient.'

'The Davies Advice Bureau at your service.'

'Do you remember how we met?'

'I'll never forget it, Karlene.'

'You were introduced to us during a lecture and then you answered our questions. I thought you were very brave – talking so openly about your disability.'

'I'm a paraplegic,' he said with a shrug. 'No use denying it. You have to accept your limitations before you can make the most of them.'

'If only Daisy had that attitude.'

'Who's Daisy?'

'She's my problem.'

Karlene told Tony about the dificulties she'd been experiencing with Daisy. He listened attentively and when she'd finished, he nodded.

'I've seen it happen before,' he said. 'Many times. When you go through such a life-changing experience – like paralysis, or an amputation – it takes away all your confidence. You're left feeling in a complete daze.'

'How do you get over that?'

'With the help of the physio department, for a start.'

'Daisy won't let us get close to her at all.'

'Then you have to get through her defences.'

'I did manage to, once,' said Karlene, wistfully.

'Then it could happen again. If you prepare her.'

'If only I knew how, Tony.'

He caught hold of the wheels of his chair and spun himself round three times, like a giant top Karlene stood back in surprise.

'It helps me to think when I do that,' Tony said, grinning at her.

'And what have you decided?'

'Bring her down here, Karlene. If she sees the disabilities that some of us have to cope with, she might begin to realize the things which people can still enjoy doing, in spite of their handicaps.'

'And will you talk to her, Tony?'

'Of course I will.'

'Thank you. I can't tell you how relieved you've made me feel.'

'My pleasure. Daisy sounds as if she needs a lot of help.'

'She does,' agreed Karlene. 'So does her mother. They're both suffering, as you can imagine. I must try and find a way to bring them back together again. Until Daisy's made it up with her mother, the real healing can't begin.'

Mark reluctantly agreed to help her. Bella had insisted on seeing her special patient again. After the shock of discovering what had really happened at Gallagher Road, she just had to speak to Jamie. They chose a moment when Sister Judd had been called away from Mendip Ward and Mark could act as a lookout. Bella hurried through the ward and into the private unit. She tapped on the door before letting herself into Jamie's room.

Jamie was sitting in an armchair by the bed. His dressing gown was draped around his shoulders, concealing the plaster cast on his arm. He smiled as she let herself into his room.

'Bella! How nice to see you!'

'Good morning, Jamie.'

'You look upset. Is anything the matter?'

'Yes,' she said, plunging straight in. 'I went to Gallagher Road last night.'

'You did – why?'

'Just out of interest; I wanted to see where you live.'

'*Did* live,' he said, ruefully. 'I won't be going back there in a hurry, I can tell you.'

'Is it true that someone tried to blow you up?'

'Who told you that?' he asked.

'A policeman on duty outside your house. They

were still sifting through the debris for clues.'

Anger flashed in his eyes, but he quickly controlled himself. He gave a wry smile, then squeezed her arm affectionately with his free hand.

'I was hoping to protect you from all that, Bella. I didn't want you to get upset.'

'Who would do that to you, Jamie?'

'It doesn't matter now.'

'But it *does*. They should be locked up!'

'They will be,' he assured her. 'When they're caught. Ron Foxwell told me the police have got several leads, and he's certain they'll track them down soon. I'd prefer to leave it to them and try and forget the whole thing.'

'You can't just shrug it off like that.'

'Why not?'

'Because they might try to murder you again,' she gasped.

'I'll be on my guard next time,' he said, firmly. Jamie tried to sound more relaxed. 'Besides, I'll be leaving here soon and going to a safer place.'

'Where's that?'

'It's a secret, Bella.'

'Even from me?'

'Just for the time being, yes.'

'But how will I know where you are?'

'I'll keep in touch, Bella,' he promised, 'and I can send you your ticket through the post.'

'Ticket?'

'Yes, you remember – for that trip to Paris.'

'Is that still on, then?' she said, uncertainly.

'Of course. I'll pick you up at the airport.'

'When will we go?'

'When my arm's out of plaster and I'm fully recovered.'

'And when those men have been caught by the police.'

'Don't even think about them.'

'I can't help it, Jamie. Someone tried to kill you – it's frightening. Don't you have any idea who they are?'

'Yes, Bella, I do. They're business rivals of mine.'

'Is *this* the way they do business?' she asked, pointing at Jamie's injuries.

'I'm afraid so,' he said, quietly. 'There was this big deal we were planning last month. If they could have pulled it off, they'd have stood to make a fortune. But I came in at the last moment and snatched it away from them.'

'Is that what this is all about? Revenge?'

'Yes, that's it, Bella.'

'Have you given their names to the police?'

'Of course I have. But they won't have been directly involved. They'll have hired other people to plant that bomb, believe me.'

Bella shivered. 'How horrible!'

'I'm trying to put it all behind me now.'

'But I had no idea your work was so dangerous.'

'It's not, Bella. Most of the time I do civilized deals with civilized people. These two were exceptions.' He patted her arm again. 'Don't worry. There's no danger now. I'll be fine.'

'Are you sure, Jamie?'

'Absolutely.'

'You could always ask for police protection.'

'I prefer to handle things my way,' he said, getting irritable. He forced a smile. 'I thought we were friends, Bella, so have a bit of faith in me.'

'OK.' She smiled. 'Especially in Paris.'

'You have to do a favour for me first, remember?'

'Of course!'

'And no questions asked, OK?'

'No questions.'

Feeling reassured, she looked at him admiringly. Jamie seemed so in control. She'd been wrong to worry unnecessarily. In future she really would have faith in him. Bella was about to apologize for her earlier doubts, when there was a sharp knock on the door.

'That's Mark!' she said. 'Somebody must be coming.'

'You'd better go, then.'

'See you again soon, Jamie.'

'I hope so, honey.'

He blew her a kiss and she smiled at him again.

As she opened the door and let herself out, Jamie's face hardened. Using his free hand, he punched the arm of the chair.

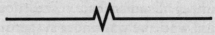

Damian looked more despondent than ever. He stirred his coffee slowly but made no attempt to drink it.

'I just couldn't keep away from the place,' he said.

'That's understandable,' said Suzie, sitting opposite him.

'I hadn't realized just how much it meant to me.'

'This hospital is much more than a place of work.'

'Yes, Suzie. I'll be devastated if I lose my job.'

'That won't happen, Damian, I'm sure it won't.'

'It's quite likely, though. If the Board of Inquiry didn't think I was guilty, why would they have suspended me from my duties?'

'That's probably normal procedure, Damian.'

'I doubt it.'

'Try and look on the bright side.'

'There isn't a bright side.' He decided to be more positive. 'Sorry, Suzie. I didn't mean to cry into my coffee. You're right. I've got to take an optimistic view. Perhaps they won't sack me after all.'

'I'm sure they won't.'

'I'll just be demoted to hospital porter.'

They laughed. Suzie was surprised to see him in the canteen. Damian had vowed not to visit the hospital while he was under suspension – but it seemed to draw him back. But she was glad to be able to boost his confidence.

'How's my other little problem?' he asked.

'What other problem?'

'Bella, of course.'

'Ah,' said Suzie. 'Still there, I'm afraid.'

'Is she speaking to you yet?'

'We had a few polite words last night.'

'Did you mention me?'

'No. I thought it best to keep off the subject.'

'Very wise, Suzie.'

'She's cooled down a bit now, that's the main thing.'

'Good. Talking to Bella when she's really angry is like walking into a fiery furnace.'

'You keep your head down,' she suggested, putting a hand on his arm. 'I'll take any aggro from Bella.'

'Thanks, Suzie.'

They were leaning close to each other, their shoulders touching, when a sharp voice made them jump and spring apart.

'Well, well! You're at it again!'

Bella was right behind them with her tray of food.

'Hi, B...Bella!' stammered Damian. 'Come and join us.'

'No, thank you! I know when three's a crowd!'

'Don't be silly, Bella,' said Suzie. 'Sit down, please.'

'Not with you two – it would put me off my food.'

'But I want to talk to you,' said Damian.

'Talk to your beloved girlfriend instead,' snapped Bella. 'I came over to apologize for getting the wrong end of the stick, and what do I find? You can't keep your hands off each other!'

'Stop yelling, Bella,' said Suzie. 'Everyone's watching!'

'Let them watch, see if I care!'

Before they could stop her, Bella had tipped the entire contents of her tray all over Damian.

He felt thoroughly humiliated.

───────────∧∨───────────

They had rehearsed their plan a couple of times. Gordy was certain it would work, but Jessica was sceptical.

'I've tried to sneak past him before,' she said, 'but he's caught me every time.'

'But you were on your own before.'

'That's true.'

'He won't be expecting a couple,' Gordy reminded her.

'It's worth a try, I suppose.'

'Trust me! My plan is foolproof,' he said. 'I promised to get you up to Carlton Ward, and I will. Scouts' honour!'

'You're wonderful, Gordy!'

She gave him a hug and he beamed with delight. It was a long time since any girl had embraced him so warmly. He felt a pang of envy. Kish was a lucky guy.

'Ready, Jessica?'

'Yes.'

'Let's go for it!'

They approached the main entrance from an angle so they couldn't be seen from within through the glass doors. Gordy put an arm round Jessica and she leaned on his shoulder. As they walked through the waiting room, he managed to screen her from view.

'There he is!' Jessica whispered.

'Where?'

'Standing by the lift.'

Kish's brother was a tall young man in a brown suit. His long black hair fell to his shoulders and his sharp eyes were scanning the waiting room. Gordy kept Jessica well-hidden and guided her towards the stairs. But it wasn't until they reached the first floor that they dared to relax.

'We did it!' she said, triumphantly.

'I knew my plan would work.' Gordy grinned broadly.

'You're a real friend, Gordy!'

She gave him an even bigger hug as, basking in their success, they went up to the second floor and walked towards Carlton Ward. Gordy was still congratulating himself on his skill in dodging the first obstacle when they ran into a second one.

Sister Russell was a slim woman of medium height with auburn hair brushed back from her face. As they approached she gave them a guarded smile of welcome.

'Can I help you?' she asked.

'This is Jessica Roe, she's come to visit her boyfriend,' said Gordy.

'Yes, I see.'

'His name is Kish,' she said. 'His surname is–'

'I know,' interrupted Sister Russell, 'and I'm quite aware of your name as well, Miss Roe. Unfortunately, I have to turn down your request. I'm afraid I can't let you into Carlton Ward.'

'Why not?' asked Gordy.

'Kish is dying to see me,' added Jessica.

'That's not what he told me,' said the Sister. 'He left specific instructions that he would only receive visits from members of his family. He doesn't want to see you, I'm afraid, dear.'

'But he must,' wailed Jessica. 'He's my boyfriend!'

'Please let Jessica in, Sister,' urged Gordy.

'I'm afraid I can't,' said Sister Russell. 'My

first duty is to the patient. I can't have someone in my care upset by unwelcome visitors.'

Jessica was shaking all over. 'I know Kish wants me, he really does!'

'That's not what he told me, Miss Roe. I'm sorry. But I'll have to ask you to leave. You really can't come in here.'

Gordy was puzzled. He turned to Jessica for an explanation but she was in no condition to give one. Trembling with emotion, she burst into tears and flung herself into his arms.

***

While one ward was rejecting a visitor, another was allowing one in. It made Bella's eyes widen in amazement.

'Jamie's got a visitor?' she gasped.

'That's right,' confirmed Mark. 'Some chap, I don't know who he is.'

'Why didn't you tell me?'

'Because you were running an errand for Sister Judd.'

'You should have come to find me,' she chided. 'This is important. Jamie told me that nobody – nobody – should visit him. Supposing this man is one of his enemies?' She grabbed his arm. 'What did he look like?'

'I only caught a glimpse of him from the back, Bella. He was going through the door into the private unit.'

'Was he young, old, middle-aged?'

'Youngish, I think.'

'What was he wearing?'

'A blue suit. And he was carrying a briefcase.'

'Suppose he had a gun inside!' she said.

'Then we'd have heard it go off by now. Relax, will you? He might be another detective. Or one of Mr Stoddard's friends.'

Bella was worried. They were clearing a bedside cabinet in Mendip Ward after the departure of another patient. She kept glancing towards the private unit. Who *was* the mystery visitor? Why hadn't Jamie mentioned him to her?

'I must go and see Jamie!' she announced.

'That's crazy, Bella.'

'But what if Jamie's in danger?'

'He can take care of himself,' said Mark. 'One thing's certain, if you march in there now, Sister Judd will march you straight out again and back to Sister Killeen.'

Bella knew Mark was right. All she could do was watch and pray. She was on tenterhooks. When their chores were completed, they were supposed to report to the Sister again but Bella hung around beside the bed. She refused to move from the spot until she knew what was going on in Jamie's private room.

She didn't have long to wait. The door of his room finally opened and raised voices could be heard. Then the visitor came storming through the door into the main ward and forced his way between the beds. Unable to stop herself, Bella stepped out to confront him.

He was a smartly-dressed young man with a briefcase, but it was his dark glasses which puzzled her. Why was he wearing them inside the hospital? She soon got her explanation.

As she blocked his way, the visitor halted. Pulling off his glasses, he glared down at her. His face was full of anger and pain. Both eyes had purple swellings beneath them and there was a strip of plaster across one eyebrow.

'What the blazes are *you* staring at?' he demanded.

Then he pushed past her and charged out of the ward.

—⌁—CHAPTER TWELVE—⌁—

Catherine White kept tight control of her students. She encouraged them to show initiative but she supervised their projects with great care. Karlene was given more leeway than the others because her tutor recognized her natural aptitude for the job. So she was delighted when Karlene seemed to be making progress in Daisy's case; her student showed an affability that was a great asset in breaking down any reserve patients might naturally feel.

'So you think it will work, Karlene?' she asked.

'We'll never know unless we try it, Mrs White.'

'And you've briefed Tony Davies?'

'He's ready and waiting.'

'Then what's keeping you?'

'You mean – I can take Daisy down to the gymnasium now?'

'That's right. And good luck, Karlene.'

It wasn't easy to persuade Daisy to go to the gym with her and when the exercises were over, she wanted to escape from the room as usual – but Karlene finally won her over.

'I've got a surprise for you, Daisy.'

'What is it?' said the young girl.

'It won't be a surprise if I tell you.' Karlene looked mysterious.

'Where are you taking me?'

'Just wait and see, Daisy.'

'But Mum will be waiting for me.'

'It won't take long, I promise,' Karlene reassured her.

Tony Davies had timed it perfectly. As Karlene pushed Daisy into the gym, he was practising alone with a basketball. Using one hand to manoeuvre his wheelchair, he bounced the ball expertly with the other. He got within a few metres of the ring, steadied himself, then shot with both hands. The ball dropped clean through the basket.

'Well done!' said Karlene, clapping enthusiastically.

Tony pretended to be surprised to see them.

'Hi, Karlene. Who's this, then?'

'Tony, this is Daisy Collier.'

'Hi, Daisy,' he said, wheeling himself across to shake her hand. 'How long have you been coming here?'

'Too long,' Daisy looked at the floor and muttered.

'They can't get rid of me,' he boasted. 'I love it here. It's like having my own private gym.'

The ball was rolling across the floor and Tony sped off to scoop it up in his hand. Soon he was bouncing it on the floor again. Karlene watched admiringly but Daisy was looking at the blanket around his legs.

'Is Tony a double amputee?' she whispered.

'No, he's a paraplegic,' explained Karlene.

'I don't know what that means,' said Daisy.

'It means he's paralysed from the waist down.'

'You mean...?'

'He has no movement at all, Daisy.'

'Was he born like that?'

'No,' said Karlene. 'Tony was a keen rugby player. That's how he finished up a wheelchair – an accident on the pitch. He'll never walk again.'

As if in defiance of the fact, Tony swung himself in a circle then stopped to attempt a difficult throw from a wide angle. His aim was perfect. The ball dropped straight through the basket. Caught up in it all, even Daisy clapped this time.

Tony retrieved the ball and held it out to her.

'Your turn now...'

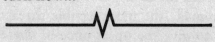

By the time he brought the drinks over, Jessica had stopped crying. She fell on her glass of wine and took a good, long sip. Gordy was relieved. When he'd brought her into the pub, she was crying and she'd attracted some strange looks from the other customers. They obviously thought he had upset Jessica and now he sat beside her and lifted his own glass.

'Cheers!' he said.

'Cheers!' she said. 'And thanks.'

'For what? The mission failed.'

'You got me up to Carlton Ward. That's all you offered to do. I'll always be grateful to you for that.'

'Why didn't Kish want to see you?'

'He did,' she insisted.

'That's not what the Ward Sister thought,' said Gordy.

'His family had got to her. *They* made her keep me out, not Kish. He'd never refuse to see me.'

'How long have you two been friends?'

'It's almost a year now.'

'Even though his family objected?'

'He never told them about me. They thought he was taking out a Bangladeshi girl. Then, one day, his brother saw us getting on a bus together. And that was that.'

'What did the family do?'

'They made the most terrible threats. He was ordered to give me up at once or there'd be big trouble.'

'And did Kish do what they told him?'

She laughed. 'No. He said he would, then went on seeing me in secret. That was fantastic.'

'Why?'

'I suppose it was the sense of danger.'

'Forbidden fruit and all that, eh?' said Gordy, fascinated.

'Yes,' she said. 'We had special times and places where we'd meet. Nobody ever knew. It was great!'

'Then what?'

'Kish had this problem with his foot. A bone malformation that can be corrected with surgery. Only because it wasn't a vital operation, he had to wait years to get in. That's when I stopped hiding.'

'And his brother saw you here?'

'Yes,' she said. 'And he put two and two together. And they made sure I was kept out.'

Though Gordy felt sorry for her, he wasn't certain she was telling him the whole story. There was no doubting her commitment to her boyfriend but Gordy wanted to hear how Kish felt about her.

'What am I going to do?' she asked, plaintively.

'Become a naturalized Bangladeshi?' he joked.

'I'd do it! If it meant I'd got Kish back, I'd do it tomorrow.'

'The first thing you should do is try and contact him. Have you tried ringing him?'

'Several times. They refuse to put me through.'

'Why?'

'I'm not close family.'

'In that case, write a letter.'

'It would never reach him, Gordy. The family would intercept it and I couldn't bear that. The thought of them reading something as private as that, well...'

'There's only one answer, then, deliver the letter to him by hand.'

'I can't get anywhere near Kish.'

Gordy sipped his beer and grinned broadly.

'You can't,' he said. 'But I bet I could.'

She was touched. 'Would you do that for *me*?'

'If it helps the course of true love.'

'Oh, Gordy! You're an angel!'

She leaped up from her seat to kiss him full on the lips. He began to wish he'd made his offer sooner.

———————————⋀⋁—————————————

Bella lingered outside Mendip Ward but it was a waste of time. Mark tugged at her elbow.

'Come on,' he said. 'We finish early today.'

'I need to see Jamie again.'

'Not a chance!'

'Sister Judd can't stay on duty for ever.'

'She doesn't, Bella. But when she knocks off, someone else takes over and they'll stop you getting into him.'

She gave a big sigh and allowed herself to be pulled towards the lift. It was so frustrating. Jamie was less than ten metres away yet she couldn't reach him. And Mark couldn't understand her desperation.

'I thought he explained everything to you.'

'He did.'

'So what's bugging you now?'

'That visitor.'

'I didn't hear any gunshot.'

'Mark!'

'Why get so worked up about it?' he said. 'The man was a friend of Jamie's. Otherwise he wouldn't have been allowed to visit him.'

'If he was a friend, why did they have a huge row?'

'Because that's what friends do – look at you and Damian.'

'He's no friend of mine!'

'But you see my point? Friends fall out and they shout at each other.'

'Not when someone's recovering from an attempt on his life, Mark. And that man's face...'

'Maybe he walked into a lamppost or something.'

'He had two black eyes. Someone had obviously beaten him up.'

'You don't *know* that, Bella.'

'I didn't like that man. He was creepy.'

Mark said nothing until they'd reached the ground floor. Then he drew Bella aside into a quiet corner.

'Do you want my honest opinion?' he said.

'Of course.'

'Promise you won't go off the deep end?'

'Why should I?'

'Because I might say something about your friend that you don't like. I know how fond you are of him.'

'Go on, Mark.'

'OK. Here goes. I think he's taking you for a ride, Bella,' he said. 'Why did he pick you when he has at least six trained nurses to choose from in this ward and his own nurse in that private room?'

'But he prefers me, Mark!'

'But why? He finds you very attractive, I'm sure. Most guys do. But there's more to it than that.'

'Is there?' she said, her eyes narrowing.

'You're only a student nurse, Bella. Like me. You're young and inexperienced. To put it bluntly, you're an easier target for an operator like Mr Jamie Stoddard.'

'I don't know what you're talking about. He's not an "operator"!'

'Then why is he mixed up with shady characters?'

'He said he had jealous business rivals.'

'What about that visitor with the dark glasses? Was he a jealous business rival as well?' He took her by the shoulders. 'Get real, Bella. Someone tries to kill him; the friend who visits him has been beaten up. Doesn't that tell you something about the sort of person he is?'

'Leave me alone,' she said, pushing him away.

'I knew you'd be angry.'

'Jamie is a good friend.'

'I'll say no more, then.'

'You've said enough already, Mark. We're nurses. We're supposed to care for our patients, not let them down. Jamie was almost killed in that explosion, and that means he gets my full sympathy. I can't believe you're criticising him like this. You've never even met him properly.'

'I can't say I'm sorry about that.'

'Well, you're wrong. He's a wonderful person. He's the best thing that's happened to me in ages. And I won't hear a word against him. Have you got that?'

'Yes,' he said, wearily. 'I've got it.'

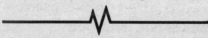

Daisy was putting every ounce of her strength into the throw. Holding the basketball against her chest, she thrust her hands forwards sending it rising up towards the metal ring. But it hit the edge and bounced off. She was deflated.

'I'll never be able to do it!' she sighed.

'You're getting better all the time,' said Tony.

'No, I'm not. I'm getting worse. My arms are hurting and I've got a pain in my back.'

'It's only a question of building up your strength,' said Karlene, encouragingly. 'That's what Tony did, didn't you?'

'Yup,' he agreed. 'It took me months.'

'Who wants to play basketball, anyway?' Daisy said with scorn. 'It's a stupid game!'

Karlene glanced at Tony. Daisy had had enough of the gym. It was time to change the conversation.

'Right,' said Tony. 'I'm off. Don't want to miss my favourite TV programme.'

'Daisy must go as well,' said Karlene. 'Her mum will be wondering what's happened to her.'

'Don't bother about Mum,' sneered Daisy.

'Why not?'

'Because I don't.'

'Of course you do,' said Tony. 'Everybody cares about their mother. I know I do. My mum is great.'

'Well, mine's not,' said Daisy.

'She's just trying to do her best,' soothed Karlene.

'You don't know her like I do.'

'Your mother's doing everything she can to help you, Daisy.'

'Then why doesn't she just keep out of my way?' she said, angrily.

Tony was shocked. 'That's a terrible thing to

say about your mum. She's the one who looks after you, Daisy.'

'That's why I hate her.'

'You can't really mean that,' said Karlene.

'Yes I can,' she continued, working herself up into a state. 'If it wasn't for her, I wouldn't be in here. She did this to me and now I'm trapped at home with her. It's awful. I hate her, I hate myself, I hate my life. I wish that lorry had run me over and killed me!'

She banged the arms of her wheelchair with her fists. 'I hate sitting in this thing all day long.'

Suddenly, Daisy threw herself forwards and lay sprawled across the floor of the gym.

CHAPTER THIRTEEN

When Suzie got home that evening, she found Bella sitting alone in the kitchen. She was spreading marmalade on a piece of toast. She looked quite calm for once and it was too good an opportunity to miss.

'Where are the others?' asked Suzie, casually.

'Gordy's in the bath, Karlene's not back yet.'

'What about Mark?'

'Up in his room,' said Bella. 'Just as well, I'm not speaking to him at the moment!'

'That makes two of us then. At this rate, you'll run out of people to talk to.'

Bella smiled faintly and bit into her toast.

'What kind of a day have you had?' asked Suzie.

'A long one.'

'I know the feeling.' She sat down. 'What's this about you falling out with Mark?'

'He said some nasty things about a friend of mine.'

'That doesn't sound like Mark. He's usually tactful.'

'Not this time, Suzie.'

She munched in silence for a while. Suzie couldn't feel any anger directed towards her now. Bravely, she broached a sensitive subject.

'I'm sorry about lunch time,' she said.

'Lunch time?'

'Damian.'

'Oh, yes! I'd forgotten him.'

'He's not likely to forget you in a hurry, Bella. You tipped your tuna salad and orange juice all over him.'

Bella giggled. 'Don't forget the apple pie and cream. That was supposed to have been my dessert.'

'All he was doing was *chatting* to me.'

'I know and I feel very guilty about that. When I see Damian again, I'll apologize to him.'

'You're not mad at us any more?'

'No. I've decided to be philosophical, Suzie. If you want him – take him.'

'But I don't "want" him.'

'Oh, come on,' said Bella. 'A kiss on the doorstep, a squeeze on the arm in the canteen. All those other little moments you must have had together.'

'There haven't *been* any.'

'I'm not jealous any more. Damian's all yours.'

'But I don't even fancy him.'

'Fine. Keep him as an escort until you meet someone you do fancy. Do what you like. It doesn't bother me.'

'Well, I'm glad to hear that, anyway.'

'It's safe to eat in the canteen again. I won't attack either of you. In fact, I'm grateful to you for taking him off my hands.'

'What do you mean?'

'I've found someone else, Suzie.'

'At the hospital?'

'Yes, he makes Damian look like a beginner.'

'Who *is* this hunk?'

'You'll see. All in good time.'

'Is it serious?'

'Dead serious,' said Bella. 'I've never met anyone quite like him. We clicked from the start. We're really great together.' She stared dreamily ahead of her. 'It's happened at last, Suzie. The real thing. I've found him.'

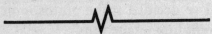

Jamie sat in bed looking down at the small package in his lap. It was covered in brown paper and sealed with Sellotape. There was a tap on the door and he slipped the package under the sheets as his nurse came in.

'Good morning, Mr Stoddard.'

'Morning.'

'How are you feeling today?'

'Restless. When are they going to let me out of this prison?'

'Ask Mr Buchanan. It's his decision.'

The nurse went through her routine and made notes on the record sheet at the end of his bed. As soon as she left, he used his free hand to take out the package. He fondled it with reverence. A telephone rang on his bedside table.

Picking up the receiver, he spoke warily into it.

'Yes?'

'Is that you, Jamie?' said a gruff voice.

'How did you get this number?' he demanded.

A throaty laugh came down the line. 'We just wanted to let you know that we're thinking about you.'

Jamie slammed down the receiver. He grabbed the package and hid it under the sheets again. It was time to do some very hard thinking.

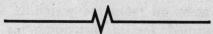

Gordy came out of the lecture theatre and walked down to the entrance hall. Jessica was there, waiting for him. She looked quite stunning in a green dress which matched the colour of her eyes. Gordy felt great as she ran over to give him a kiss. There was a murmur of envious remarks from the other guys around him. Jessica made him feel special.

'I've got it,' she said.

'Got what?'

'The letter.'

She produced it from her bag and handed it to him. As he felt the weight of it, he raised an eyebrow.

'Bit on the long side, isn't it?'

'No,' she said. 'Only fifteen pages.'

'That's not a letter – it's a novel!'

'Just give it to Kish, please!'

'I will, don't worry.'

'And make sure you wait for a reply.'

'But it'll take him a week to read it!'

Jessica grinned. 'You're so funny, Gordy. And so kind. I'll never forget what you've done for us. Kish's family are trying to keep us apart and you're going to bring us together again.'

'I'm quite happy to play Cupid.'

'You're a real friend!'

She kissed him full on the lips and loud whistles went up from the watching students. Gordy beamed. Jessica was doing his image a power of good.

'I liked you from the moment we met,' she confided.

'Did you?'

'Yes. It was because you were wearing those shorts.'

'I'd been jogging – from home to the hospital.'

'They really turned me on.'

'My shorts?'

'No, stupid. Your legs. They're dead sexy.'

Gordy blossomed. 'Do you really think so?'

'I know so,' said Jessica. 'If I wasn't madly in love with Kish, I'd be chasing after you.'

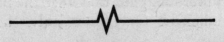

During their mid-morning break, Mark finally managed to speak to Bella. His tone was apologetic.

'I'm sorry about what I said, Bella.'

'So you should be.'

'You're entitled to choose your own friends.'

'Exactly.'

'I just hope I can be one of them again.'

She smiled. It was the first sign of a thaw. Bella's manner towards him had been icy until then.

'You can't go on dodging me,' he said. 'We're supposed to be working together in Mendip Ward.'

'I know.'

'So are we on speaking terms again?'

Bella thought it over. 'All right,' she said. 'But only if you help me to see him again.'

'Isn't that a bit risky?'

'I *must*, Mark. Can't you understand that?'

It was hopeless. She wouldn't listen to his warnings. He consoled himself with the thought that Jamie Stoddard would soon be released from hospital. Sighing, Mark gave in to her request.

'I'll help,' he said.

Their opportunity soon came. Two of the cubicles at the end of Mendip Ward were vacated and they were assigned to change the bed linen. They completed the task quickly, then Bella slipped off into the private unit.

Jamie was relieved to see her.

'Thank goodness you've come, Bella!'

'I was worried about you,' she said.

'Why?'

'That strange visitor you had.'

'Oh – forget him.'

'Who was he, Jamie?'

'Just a former business colleague,' he said, airily.

'I heard you arguing with him.'

'Yes, I was sending him packing. He let me down over a deal, so I won't be doing any business with him again.'

'What happened to his face?'

'I told you. Forget him. He's history.' Jamie was looking irritated by her questions.

'If you say so.'

'I do, Bella,' he said, firmly.

Jamie looked tense and threatened. Bella had never seen him like that before. An anxious came into her eyes and he made an effort to compose himself.

'Have you missed me?' he teased.

'Like crazy!'

'I missed you, too.'

'Is that the truth?'

'Of course. You're the one person in this hospital I can trust. That means a lot to me, Bella.'

'Great.'

'And I won't forget that trip to Paris. What would you like to see? The Eiffel Tower? I'll take you right to the top.'

'I'd love that, Jamie.'

'We'll see all the sights.'

'I can't wait.'

'You'll have to, I'm afraid,' he said, a cautious note coming into his voice. 'I need to recover properly and to...sort out a few business problems.'

'Have the police caught those men yet?'

'What men?'

'The ones who put a bomb in your house, Jamie.'

'Just put them out of your mind.'

'How can I? If they're still after you...'

'Do as I tell you!' he snapped.

Jamie's anger made her take a step back, but he was immediately apologetic. Beckoning to her to come nearer, he held out his free hand.

'Sorry, Bella. This place is getting to me.'

'You frightened me for a moment, Jamie.'

'I won't do it again, I promise. The truth is, I hate being locked up. This room is like a prison cell. I just have to get out of here.' He squeezed her hand again. 'When we meet outside this hospital, it will all be very different.'

'I hope so, Jamie.'

'I'll show you how grateful I really am.'

Bella warmed to him all over again.

'Let's not waste time now, though,' he said, briskly. 'Remember I asked you to do a big favour for me? Well, this is it.'

He reached under his sheet and took out the brown – paper package. After staring at it for a moment, he gave it to her.

'What is it?' she asked, surprised.

'Something really important to me.'

'What do you want me to do?'

'Just keep it safe until I get out.'

'Why can't it stay here?'

'You promised you'd ask no questions, Bella.'

'OK. Sorry, Jamie.'

'Now,' he said, sternly, 'do you have somewhere in your house where it can be locked away safely?'

'Yes – in my room.'

'Nobody else must see it, Bella.'

'Don't worry, they won't.'

'And you mustn't open it,' he warned. 'It's a kind of test; do this big favour for me and you'll get everything I promised you. If you let me down...'

'I won't!' she affirmed. 'You can count on me.'

A look of relief flooded into his face.

'Just wait until we get to Paris!' he said.

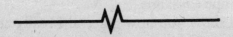

Suzie was crossing the car park when she saw him.

'Damian!' she called.

'Oh hi, Suzie.'

He walked slowly towards her, looking around him in as he did so. He stopped while he was still a few metres away from her and held out his arm.

'What's the matter?' she said.

'I don't want Bella to catch us together for the *third* time. Goodness knows what she might tip over me next.'

'Relax, Damian. She's forgiven you.'

'There was nothing to forgive.'

'We know that, but she doesn't. Anyway, she's backed off, Bella's talking to us again; peace has been restored.'

'That's great news.'

'And she's got a new guy in her life.'

'Fantastic!' Damian stopped glancing over his shoulder and walked closer to her.

'I've got a piece of news for you now, Suzie.'

'Oh yes, what is it?'

'One of the charges against me has been dropped.'

'Damian, that's wonderful!'

'Mr Mullins has decided not to sue me over the drug dose I prescribed for his son. He saw there was no chance of a clear-cut victory, so he changed his mind.'

'You're going to be OK. I told you.'

'I'm not sure yet.'

'There's only one charge to face now.'

'Yes,' he said. 'But it's the most serious one. I *should* have picked up that rib damage, Suzie. I did examine the boy – but I missed it. How would you like to be rushed in to Casualty to find yourself in the hands of an inexperienced, incompetent doctor.'

'You're not incompetent, Damian.'

'I was under such pressure that night.'

'Well, you must make that point to the Board of Inquiry.'

'It might not help me.'

'What do you mean?'

'We're supposed to be able to handle pressure, Suzie. If you can't do that, you shouldn't be working in Casualty. We deal with life-and-death situations every day. I think they're going to throw the book at me.'

'They wouldn't dare do that!'

'Yes they would.' He looked around sadly. 'I'm going to miss this place. I've tried to be optimistic but I've got this feeling in my bones. The Board of Inquiry's going to make an example of me. I'll be kicked out of the hospital.'

Bella spent the rest of the morning in a state of apprehension. The package just fitted into the pocket of her nurse's uniform but it felt heavy. She was terrified that Sister Judd would spot it and ask her what she was carrying. As soon as her lunch break came, she headed for the lift.

Mark tried hard to keep up with her.

'What's the big rush?' he said.

'I have to get back to the house.'

'What about lunch?'

'I'll grab an apple or something.'

'You need a proper meal, Bella.'

'I have to do something more important that think about food,' she told him.

Mark didn't dare to question her further. He could see she was quite jumpy. He went off to the canteen as usual as she headed for the main exit. Bella was soon walking quickly along the pavement with one hand holding tightly to the package in her pocket – as though it was the most precious thing in her possession.

By the time she got to the house, she was out of breath. It was only when she was inside her room that she dared to relax. She turned the key in the lock and sat down on her bed. As she took out the package, a thrill went through her. It was the thought of Jamie's trust in her that excited her.

Her room was small and very untidy. There were any number of potential hiding places and she tried each of them in turn. The wardrobe was an obvious place and at first she hid the package behind her dresses. Then she put it in the hatbox on top of the wardrobe. Her next choice was the small cupboard in the corner – and so it went on.

When she'd exhausted all the other possibilities, she settled for the one that had first occurred to her. Kneeling down, she pulled out a large suitcase from beneath her bed. It was always kept locked and contained a few trinkets and a collection of love letters from her various admirers.

Bella decided that the package was a kind of love letter. At least it was proof of Jamie's affection for her. When he'd needed someone to do him a favour, he'd chosen her. It made her feel special. He really must care about her.

She found her key and unlocked the case. As the lid flipped up, she saw her scattering of treasures. She placed the package carefully in the middle of them. It was then that her curiosity got the better of her.

What could be in the brown paper? Why did it have to be smuggled out? Couldn't it be kept just as safely at the hospital? Jamie had sworn her to secrecy, but for what reason? And just how important was the package to him?

Questions she'd never thought of before began to flood into her mind. If it was so vital to put it in her safekeeping, why hadn't he given it to her earlier? Soon, the temptation to open the package was almost irresistible. If she could just peel back a corner and peep inside, the mystery might be explained.

Bella grabbed it and put in her lap. But a warning bell had sounded inside her head. No questions. Jamie would know if his package had been tampered with and he would be furious. If she really wanted to know what was in it, she would just have to wait until he decided to tell her.

Mastering her impatience, she put the package back in the case and shut the lid. She'd kept her part of the bargain.

On her way back to the hospital, she thought about the holiday in Paris.

───────────⋀───────────

Mrs White had invited them both into her office. Vera Collier looked more dishevelled and worried than ever but she listened attentively as Karlene told her what had happened in the gym. To spare Daisy's mother's feelings, Karlene tried to tone down what the young girl had actually said in her outburst. But Mrs Collier nodded wearily.

'Daisy hates me,' she said. 'And who can blame her?'

'We just have to help her achieve a more positive attitude,' said Mrs White. 'As physiotherapists, we can only deal with the physical problems she faces. But it's possible Daisy may need to see a psychologist.'

Mrs Collier looked alarmed. 'A psychologist?'

'With your permission, of course.'

'Well, I'm not sure about that, Mrs White.'

'It might help Daisy.'

'Are you saying there's something wrong with her mind?'

'Of course not,' said Karlene.

'A psychologist would just talk through her problems,' added Catherine White. 'Then Daisy might learn to understand them more clearly herself and be able to come to terms with them.'

'No,' she said, firmly. 'I know my daughter. She just wouldn't cooperate. The only person who's been able to get more than a sentence out of her is Karlene.'

'That's true,' said Mrs White.

'She's better than any psychologist.'

'I'm not so sure about that,' said Karlene. 'I only get through to her for a short while and then she shuts down again. I'm afraid the scene in the gym was quite scary.'

'But your visit clearly helped,' reminded her tutor. 'Daisy learned a lot from watching Tony Davies. He's fighting back against his disability.

Something of his courage may have rubbed off on her.'

'I'm sure it did,' agreed Karlene.

'Let's try and build on that, shall we?'

'How can we do that?' asked Mrs Collier.

'Karlene's got an idea about that.'

'Yes,' said Karlene. 'I have. But I need your help, Mrs Collier.'

'I'll do anything for Daisy, anything.'

'Then I want you to ring Daisy's school...'

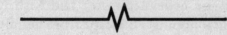

Gordy went up to Carlton Ward that afternoon. Sister Russell was in her office, talking to one of her nurses. Gordy slipped past and into the ward. He picked Kish out immediately; he was a strikingly handsome young man with the same shoulder-length hair as his brother. Kish was lying on his bed with his bandaged foot up in a sling. He was reading a computer magazine.

Gordy hurried over to him and spoke in a whisper.

'Kish?'

'That's me.'

'I'm Gordy Robbins.'

'Yes, what can I do for you?'

'Look, this is for you, could you take it?' said Gordy, pulling the letter out from under his coat. 'Special delivery.'

'Who from?'

'Jessica Roe.'

'Oh no!' wailed Kish. 'Not again!'

Gordy was staggered. 'Don't you want to read her letter?'

'No, thanks. I know exactly what it'll say.'

'But she's your girlfriend, isn't she, Kish?'

'She was, but not any more. I told her it was all over.'

'That's not what Jessica says. According to her, you're lying in here, desperate to see her.'

'Don't you believe it, mate,' said Kish. 'I came into hospital hoping I'd escape from her. But no – Jessica just won't be shaken off. I've had to ask my brother to stay on guard duty to keep her out.'

'Jessica said your family was keeping you apart.'

'That's rubbish. They liked Jessica. So did I – at first. Then she got a bit too serious.'

Gordy felt rather foolish. He'd been sent on a mission without knowing the whole story. Kish wouldn't even look at the fifteen-page letter.

'Is there any reply?' asked Gordy.

'Yes,' said Kish. 'Break it to her as gently as you can, please. It's all over. We had some great times, but I want out. Pestering me won't get her anywhere. Please try to make Jessica understand that, will you?'

'I don't think it'll be easy.'

Gordy liked him. Kish was clearly telling the truth. He still had a lot of affection for Jessica but didn't want such a close relationship with her, or anyone, just yet. Instead of being the pining boyfriend she described, Kish was a sensible young man trying to get away from her over-eager passions.

'Well,' said Gordy. 'I promised I'd bring the letter.'

'Throw it in the bin, will you?' suggested Kish.

'I might just do that.'

'While you're at it, do the same with these.'

Kish opened his bedside cabinet and a dozen unopened envelopes fell out. Gordy recognized the handwriting immediately. They were all letters from Jessica.

'Get her off my back, Gordy,' said Kish. '*Please!*'

———————/\/———————

Bella was dying to speak to Jamie again but she couldn't get near him. She wanted to reassure him that his package was safe and that she'd followed his instructions. She knew he'd be extremely pleased with her and she longed to bask in his gratitude – but there was no hope of that. Sister Judd had given her an endless stream of chores. Bella had hardly had a moment to snatch a word with Mark.

'I must see him again,' she whispered.

'Well, you'll have to do it without my help, Bella.'

'Mark!'

'Sorry, but Sister Judd wants me to help serve tea to the patients. I'll be tied up for the best part of an hour.'

Bella stamped her foot. She felt frustrated and angry.

When she'd finished her jobs, she went back down the ward to the Sister's office. It was empty; she felt hopeful. Now Bella wondered if she should risk a lightning visit to the private unit. One minute alone with Jamie was better than nothing.

But before she could move, she heard a voice ring in her ear.

'Excuse me. Is this Mendip Ward?'

'Yes,' said Bella.

'I've got the right place, then.'

The visitor was an attractive woman in her twenties. She wore a neat grey suit with a brooch on one lapel. She was of medium height, but her poise and confident manner made her seem taller.

'I believe you have a private unit here,' she said.

'That's right. At the far end of the ward.'

'In that case, I'll find my own way.'

'I'm afraid you can't go in there,' said Bella, obstructing her path. 'We only have one patient and he doesn't allow any visitors.'

'Excuse me, out of my way, please. I wish to speak to him.'

'I'm afraid he's left strict instructions – he doesn't want to see anyone.'

'Out of my way, young lady!'

Sister Judd came up in time to overhear this exchange.

'What's going on here, Nurse Denton?'

'This lady wants to visit our private patient, Sister.'

'Oh?' said Sister Judd. 'My understanding is that he doesn't wish to see anybody.'

'Oh he'll want to see me,' asserted the visitor. 'My name is Carolyn Stoddard. I'm Jamie's sister.'

Sister Judd was impressed. 'I see.'

'He never mentioned a sister to me,' said Bella.

'Keep out of this, Nurse Denton.'

'But Jamie doesn't want *any* visitors, Sister.'

'Exceptions are made for close family.'

'Thank you,' said the woman, loftily. 'May I go in?'

'Of course. It's the first room on the right.'

'Please stop her, Sister Judd,' said Bella.

'I told you to keep out of this, Nurse.'

'But I don't trust her, Sister!'

'Would you please ask this young lady to stand aside so that I can visit my brother?' said the woman, pointedly. 'I had no idea that it would be such a difficult exercise.'

Sister Judd glared at Bella.

'Nurse Denton'

'Yes, Sister?'

'Please let this lady pass.'

'Sister, please, just ask her for proof of identity.'

'Out of my way!' This time the woman shouted.

Sister Judd pulled Bella's elbow and she was pushed aside as the visitor clacked down the ward on her high heels. Bella felt crazy with frustration – but there was nothing that she could do.

'Nurse Denton!' said Sister Judd. 'Two of my part-timers are returning to work tomorrow. I will have no further need for you and Nurse Andrews.'

'Please, Sister, you can't send me away from Mendip Ward!'

'I can and I will. Not before time, in my view!'

Bella was mortified. She looked down the ward in consternation. When she saw the visitor tap on Jamie's door and let herself in, she felt as if her world had stopped spinning.

Gordy took Jessica to the gardens so that he could pass on Kish's message in private. They sat on a bench in the sunshine with Jessica buzzing with impatience.

'Well?' she said. 'Did you see Kish?'

'Yes, I did.'

'And did you give him my letter?'

'I tried to, Jessica. But he wouldn't take it.'

'Why not?'

'I think you know.' Gordy leaned closer to her. 'You didn't give me all the facts, did you?'

'We love each other, that's the only fact that matters.'

'You may love Kish but he doesn't feel the same way about you.'

Her face collapsed. 'Is that what he said?'

'More or less.'

'But I *need* him!'

'That's what frightens him, I think.'

'But he worships me!'

'He did, Jessica. And with good reason – you're an amazing girl. I think he's crazy to break it off – but it's his decision.'

'Do you really mean that, Gordy?'

'Yes, Kish is the loser. No question of that.'

'Forget Kish,' she said with sudden venom.

'What?'

'He's past history. Why should I waste my time on him?'

'But you said you were crazy about him.'

'I was. More fool me! I'll stay where I'm appreciated.'

'And where's that?' he murmured.

'Right here.'

Jessica threw her arms round him and kissed

him passionately on the mouth. Gordy couldn't believe his luck. When he came up for air, he was grinning broadly.

'Didn't think my get fit campaign would work this quick!'

Jessica grabbed him again.

CHAPTER FIFTEEN

Karlene waited for Daisy to come over to her. It was important, she felt, for Daisy to make the first move. Throughout the exercise session, she had been very subdued. Karlene could see she felt embarrassed about what had happened at the gym. Now, when she'd had time to think about it, Daisy clearly didn't want to alienate her two new friends.

She wheeled herself across the room to Karlene.

'Can we go and see Tony again today?' she asked.

'If you want to, Daisy.'

'Yes, I do. I liked him a lot.'

'Wait just a minute, Daisy.'

Karlene slipped out of the room for a moment to check that her plan had been set into motion. Vera Collier had done exactly what they'd arranged so Karlene went back to collect Daisy and began to push her towards the gym.

Two men in wheelchairs were working out with weights, and a woman with an artificial arm was using it to pitch a netball. Tony was playing table tennis with a young boy who was also in a wheelchair. Daisy watched, amazed, at the speed and skill of their game.

Tony stopped playing when he saw her.

'Hi, Daisy!' he said, coming over. 'Good to see you again.'

'Hi, Tony,' said Daisy.

'Fancy a game?'

'No thanks. Not just now.'

Daisy began to shift uneasily in her chair. She wasn't used to apologizing, but she was doing her best.

'Sorry...you know...about yesterday.'

'Forget it,' said Tony, cheerfully. 'We were all a bit like that at first. I know I was.'

'Were you?' prompted Karlene.

'Yes. I was really angry. I blamed everyone else for what had happened to me – and took it out on them. Tantrums, sulks, the lot. I was a real pain in the neck.'

'How did you get over it?' asked Karlene.

'It was common sense, really. I gave myself a good talking to. The truth is, I was as much to blame for the accident as anyone else. I mean, it was my choice to play rugby that day. I was one hundred per cent a volunteer. It was just a freak accident that left me paralysed. It could have happened to someone else when that scrum collapsed. I was just unlucky.'

'Is that when you began to fight back? When you realized that?'

'You bet!' He smiled at Daisy. 'How about you?'

'Me?' She looked startled.

'When are you planning to stop blaming other people?'

Instantly, Daisy replied, 'It was Mum's fault,' she said. '*She* did this to me.'

'You mean, she pushed you off the bus?'

'Well, no...'

'Then how was it her fault?'

'She sort of...made me do it.'

'That's not true,' said Karlene, softly. 'Your mother loves you, Daisy, you know that. The last thing in the world she wanted was for you to get hurt.'

'Then why did she argue with me?'

'Why did *you* argue with with *her*?' asked Tony.

Daisy hesitated – she was confused. Until she'd met her new friends, everything had been very clear in her mind; now it was not. They were gently forcing her to look at the accident from another angle.

'Mum started the row,' she said, defensively. 'She always has a go at me. Do this, do that. She's worse than Dad used to be. Why do I have to do what *she* wants all the time? It's not fair, Mum never does anything for me!'

'Doesn't she?' said Karlene. 'Look.'

She signalled to Mrs Collier through the glass door. When she came into the gym, she was with a slim, lithe young woman, wearing a tracksuit. Daisy was quite surprised. Her visitor was Miss Whitlow, her games teacher from school.

'Hello, Daisy,' she said, with a warm smile.

'Hello, Miss Whitlow.'

Nodding a greeting to Karlene and Tony, she responded with a broad grin. The blonde and attractive Miss Whitlow seemed the epitome of physical fitness.

'Daisy, I've been meaning to come and see you,' she said. 'How are you?'

'Not too bad, Miss Whitlow.'

Daisy was torn between delight and embarrassment. She was really thrilled to have a visit from her favourite teacher, but uneasy at being seen in a wheelchair. Miss Whitlow looked round.

'This is miles better than the school gym!'

'Come and use it any time!' urged Tony.

She smiled. 'I don't think the hospital would be too pleased if I turned up with thirty-five noisy young boys and girls. Ask Daisy. She knows what some of the kids are like.'

'I certainly do!' agreed Daisy, laughing.

'Everyone's asking after you, Daisy.'

'Are they, Miss Whitlow?'

'When do you think you're coming back to school?'

Karlene winked at Tony and the two of them moved quietly away. Miss Whitlow's visit seemed to have broken through Daisy's defensive behaviour, and she was soon chatting happily with her teacher. After standing watching for a while, Mrs Collier went over and joined in their conversation. Soon, all three of them were getting on well.

'Thanks, Tony,' said Karlene.

'Bring Daisy in here any time you like,' he said. 'And the same goes for Miss Whitlow! She can come and teach me games any time!'

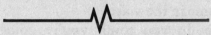

Bella was pacing restlessly up and down outside Mendip Ward.

'Come on,' said Mark. 'Let's go home.'

'Not until I see Jamie again.'

'There's no chance of that. We've finished our duties on this ward now. There's no reason for us to hang around here.'

'I'm convinced that woman wasn't Jamie's sister, Mark. I'm certain of it. He would have mentioned her to me. She had no right to force her way into his room like that.'

'I'm sure he can look after himself,' replied Mark, fed up with Bella's obsession with Jamie.

'And did you see her when she left his room?' said Bella. 'She was furious. They'd obviously had a row. What kind of a sister visits her brother in hospital just to upset him?'

'It sounds as if he was the one who upset her.'

'No, there was definitely something fishy

about her, Mark. I know it.'

'Bella,' he said, quietly. 'It's not your problem.'

'Yes, it is. Look, I can't stand the suspense any longer. I'm going to get to the bottom of this right now.'

Bella marched boldly into Mendip Ward and headed for the private unit. But Sister Judd came through the door ahead of her, and placed her ample frame in the way.

'Where do you think you're going, Nurse Denton?'

'I'd like to see Mr Stoddard, please.'

'That's impossible, you know that.'

'But I need to talk to him, Sister.'

'You need to take yourself out of Mendip Ward altogether, Nurse. You've got no reason to be here any more. As for Mr Stoddard, he's just asked me to make sure no other visitors come in to see him. And that includes you.'

'Did Jamie say that?' asked Bella, desperately.

'I'm saying it,' confirmed Sister Judd. 'And before you try to sneak in there when I'm not looking, you might as well know that his door is locked.' She held up a key before slipping it into her pocket. 'Goodbye, Nurse Denton.'

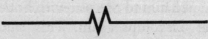

It was a mistake to mention his car. As soon as Jessica heard Gordy owned a car, she insisted on being given a ride in it. Gordy obliged at once, but the drive lasted less than five minutes. As they approached a multistorey car park, Jessica pointed to it enthusiastically.

'In there – quick!' she said.

'Why?' asked Gordy, puzzled.

'Just go up to the top floor.'

Gordy did as she asked but was still confused. The top floor was virtually empty. Why did she want him to go up there when there were vacant places on all the lower floors? As the car rolled to a halt, Jessica provided the answers.

'Come here, gorgeous! she said.

'Jessica!'

This time, Jessica really came on strong. She began to tear his coat off and her kisses were more passionate than ever. Gordy was very responsive at first – Jessica was the answer to his dreams. He couldn't believe Kish would have got rid of such a wonderful girlfriend.

It was a good ten minutes before she broke off to speak again.

'That's lovely, Gordy!' she said.

'Yes!' he gasped.

'I always dreamed of marrying a doctor!'

She pinned him to the seat with both arms and started to kiss him again. This time, Gordy began to panic. He was looking for friendship, not a life commitment. He couldn't even *think* about marriage for the next six years. In any case, Jessica wasn't quite the kind of wife he had in mind. She was too overwhelming.

As he tried to ease her away, Jessica thought he was being playful and she fought back like a tiger. It was minutes before Gordy managed to disentangle himself long enough to take a few deep breaths. But her next kiss trapped him again.

'Kish!' he said to himself. 'HELP!'

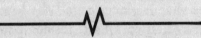

Mark argued with Bella all the way home, but to no avail. He simply could not persuade her that she would be better off without Jamie Stoddard. They were so caught up in their discussion that they didn't notice the car which had been trailing them from the hospital.

As they let themselves into the house, Mark made one last attempt to get her to see reason.

'He's been one long headache from the start, Bella.'

'That's not true, Mark.'

'It is; first thing he does is to insist on a private room. Why all the secrecy? What's he hiding from?'

'He's got enemies, Mark, I'm sure he has.'

'Exactly!'

'That man with the dark glasses was probably one of them,' she said. 'But Jamie soon got rid of him.'

'What about his "sister"? Was she another enemy?'

'She certainly wasn't a friend.'

'That's two people you have to worry about, then.'

'Me? Why me?'

'Because you're the one person he's trusted.'

'Yes, I am,' she said, proudly. 'And that's very important to me.'

'It may be important to the man in dark glasses as well, Bella. And to that woman. I told you before, being involved with Jamie Stoddard is bad news – maybe even dangerous. Suppose they come after you?'

'Why would they do that?'

'Who knows?' he said. 'To get back at him, maybe. To get information out of you. He befriended you for a good reason. I bet they'll want to know what it is.'

'Jamie *likes* me.'

'He's using you, Bella.'

'No way! I don't believe it!'

'He's getting you involved in his seedy world.'

'No, he's not,' she said, angrily. 'All I agreed to do was to look after his...'

Her voice trailed off as she realized she was breaking a confidence. Mark was on to her confession like a shot.

'He *gave* you something?' She turned away

but he took hold of her wrist. 'What was it, Bella? Tell me!'

'I can't, Mark. I promised.'

'But it could put you in serious danger!'

'Mark...'

'It could, Bella. His enemies don't mess around. They tried to kill him, remember. Why? What are they after?'

'I don't know.'

'Supposing it's the thing he gave you?'

'That's crazy!'

'Is it?'

'I'm just looking after a small package for him, that's all. There's nothing sinister in that. Now leave me alone.'

'What's in the package?' he pressed.

'How should I know, I haven't looked!'

'Why not find out now, Bella?'

They argued on and on until Bella was finally persuaded to take Mark up to her room and show him the package. She held the heavy little parcel in her hand.

'You see? It's quite harmless.'

'Then why did he need to get it out of the hospital?'

'He didn't tell me, Mark.'

'I'm sure he didn't.' He took the package. 'And I can see why. This could be a time bomb, Bella.'

'Don't be ridiculous,' she cried.

'Not a real time bomb, but something which could explode in your face, if you're not careful. Open it up, Bella.'

'No!'

'All right, then. I will.'

'No Mark! Give it to me!'

She grabbed the package but Mark resisted. There was a brief struggle and then the brown paper ripped open. Both of them stared in astonishment, rooted to the spot.

They were holding thick wads of fifty pound notes in their hands.

CHAPTER SIXTEEN

Mark was the first to recover.

'There must be thousands here, Bella!'

'I've never *seen* so much money!' she gasped.

'Now will you believe me?' He was almost shouting at her. 'Jamie Stoddard's a criminal!'

'No, No! Of course he's not!'

'But you're holding the proof in your hands, Bella.'

'I'm just holding the package he gave me to look after,' said Bella. 'He'll go mad when he knows it's been opened. It's all your fault, Mark.'

'Look, Bella, nobody keeps this amount of money in notes, Bella. I thought he told you he was an investment banker.'

'He is!'

'Then what's he doing with this?'

'I'm sure there's an explanation.'

'Yes,' said Mark, sarcastically. 'I can guess just what it is. Genuine bankers use cheque books and credit cards. Not fifty pound notes. What was he going to do? Pay his hospital bills in cash?'

Bella was upset by her discovery. It cast a real shadow over her friendship with Jamie. At the same time, she didn't want to admit that he was in the wrong. She clung to the hope that he would be able to explain everything and then they could enjoy their holiday together, in Paris.

A loud banging on the front door interrupted them.

'Who's that?' Bella looked startled.

'Hide that money away, quick,' said Mark. 'I'll go and see.'

While Bella stuffed the money back into the suitcase, Mark raced down stairs. The banging became even louder and it made him cautious. Instead of opening the door, he slipped into the living room and peered through the window. A burly man was standing there with a female companion.

Bella had run down after him and was peeping round the curtains.

'It's her!' she whispered, hoarsely.

'Who?'

'Jamie's so-called "sister". What does *she* want?'

'That package, I bet,' said Mark.

The man's fist pounded ever harder on the front door. And now the woman opened the letterbox and called through it.

'Let us in, Bella! We know you're in there! We followed you home from the hospital. We need that package that Jamie Stoddard gave you. *Now*!'

'Go away!' cried Bella, terrified.

'Let us in!'

'Go away!' said Mark. 'Or we'll call the police!'

'They'd never get here in time,' shouted the woman, threateningly. 'If you don't open this door, we'll smash our way in.'

As if to demonstrate his strength, the man hit the door with his full weight. It shuddered under the impact.

'What are we going to do?' gulped Bella, shaking.

'Make a run for it!' decided Mark. 'Go and get the money.'

He grabbed an upright chair and jammed the end of it under the doorknob as Bella raced up to her room to get the torn package. She stuffed it into her handbag as she came charging down the stairs, her heart thumping wildly.

'Where are we going?' she said.

'Out through the back!' said Mark, quickly. 'Follow me!'

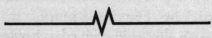

Suzie was surprised by this sudden new development.

'This evening?' she asked.

'In half an hour,' said Damian, looking dejected.

'Did the chairman of the Board of Inquiry ask for you?'

'It wasn't a request, Suzie. It was an order.'

'But why does he want to see you at such short notice?'

'To pass on bad news, I expect. That I'm out of the hospital!'

'That's crazy, Damian. You haven't even been in front of the Board yet.'

'I've got a horrible feeling I'm not going to,' said Damian. 'The chairman has probably reviewed the evidence against me and found it convincing. I made a serious mistake, Suzie. I can't pretend I didn't. There doesn't seem much point in going through with the Board of Inquiry when it's an open-and-shut case.'

'You must have a chance to defend yourself.'

'I expect the chairman will give me that this evening.'

'But they can't dismiss you without a full inquiry.'

'Oh yes, they can.'

Suzie tried to console the young doctor, but to no avail. The summons from the chairman of the Board of Inquiry seemed ominous. There was no point in deceiving himself any longer, Damian would be sacked, and that would be that.

'Thanks for your help, Suzie. It meant a lot.'

'I'll wait until you've had your meeting.'

'Don't worry,' he said. 'I'll be going straight back to my flat – to pack my bags and get out of here.'

Mark helped Bella over the wall at the end of their small back garden, then passed her bag to her. From inside the house came the sound of splintering wood. Their unwanted visitors had forced their way in. Mark didn't pause to give them a welcome! Vaulting over the wall, he grabbed Bella's hand.

'Quick!' he said. 'Run!'

'Where?' she gasped.

'To the hospital!'

They ran off down the lane which bisected the block. After a quick search of the house, their pursuers came out into the garden and they heard Mark and Bella's speeding footsteps.

They raced to look over the wall.

'Go after them!' the woman ordered the man. 'I'll get the car.'

Clambering over the wall, he gave chase.

Mark and Bella had never run so fast in their lives. It wasn't far to the hospital, but they were gasping for air by the time they reached it. The burly man was gaining on them every second and the car screeched past them and tried to cut them off. Just in time, they turned in through the gate and headed for the main entrance.

'What are we going to do?' gasped Bella.

'We'll split up,' panted Mark. 'I'll alert Security and you go up to Mendip Ward. Go to

Jamie – he's the one who got us into this mess. Hand the money back to him and get the hell out!'

Bella was given no chance to argue. As they fell into the building, Mark sped off down a corridor to the left. Bella ran through Reception and on into the waiting room. When she reached the lift, she pressed the button frantically, then turned round just as the two figures were pushing their way through the door.

The woman ran purposefully towards the lift. Breathing hard from his chase, the man lumbered after her. Bella couldn't afford to wait for the lift or they would catch her easily. She darted to the stairs and sped up them, taking three steps at a time. Her pursuers followed.

By the time she reached the fourth floor, Bella could hardly move – she gasped for air and her lungs and legs were hurting with the effort of running up the stairs so fast. Naked fear drove her on. She staggered along the corridor and into Mendip Ward. The patients sat up as they watched her lurch towards the private unit, closely followed by the strange couple.

Sister Judd was just leaving Jamie's room as Bella cannoned into her, knocking them both flying.

'What ever are you doing, girl!' asked the Sister, picking herself up.

'Where's Jamie, Sister? I must see him!'

Bella swung into his room with an irate Sister Judd at her heels. Jamie sat up in bed, alarmed.

'What's wrong? What on earth are you doing here, Bella?' he said.

'Bringing this back!'

She opened her bag to take out the torn package but she had no time to hand it over. The two chasing her barged through the open door. As they stood there swaying, trying to recover their breath, the woman pointed to the package in Bella's hand.

'We'll take that!' she ordered.

'No, you won't,' said Bella, pulling it to her chest.

But the man produced a gun, pointing it menacingly at Bella.

'Come on,' said the woman. 'Hand it over!'

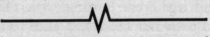

Visitors in the waiting room in Reception were still wondering what all the commotion had been about when a second chase took place. And it was just as frenetic. Gordy came sprinting through the door with a wild-eyed Jessica following him. Seeing the welcome sight of Kish's brother, Gordy dragged him from his chair and virtually threw him at his pursuer. Jessica was soon entangled with the official bodyguard.

Gordy leaped up the stairs two at a time until

he reached the second floor. A final spurt along the corridor took him to Carlton Ward, where Sister Russell saw him coming and tried to intercept him.

'Can I help you, sir?' she asked, stiffly.

'Not unless you've got a straitjacket handy!'

'A *what*?'

'Take it downstairs – she needs to be restrained.'

Gordy dodged round her and plunged on into the ward itself. Kish was still lying in bed with his leg in a sling as he went up to him. Gordy's voice had the ring of true desperation.

'Save me from Jessica!' he gasped. 'She's too hot for me to handle!'

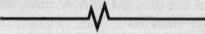

Bella was terrified. Her heart was pounding as she stared down the barrel of the gun. Sister Judd remained calm but tense and Jamie was shaking with anger.

'Don't be a fool, Mac,' he hissed. 'Put that gun down.

Now the man levelled his weapon directly at Jamie.

'I should have shot you when I had the chance – never mind the bomb. That way we'd have been sure.'

'Shut up, Mac,' said the woman. 'We want the money.'

'Hand it over!' demanded Mac.

'No!' said Bella, bravely. 'It belongs to Jamie.'

'It's ours!' rasped the woman. 'It's part of our share. Precious Jamie here tried to cheat us out of it.'

'No, I did not!' he snarled.

'Hand it over!' insisted Mac.

'Don't, Bella!' warned Jamie.

'She's got no choice,' the woman argued. 'Either we get the money now or Mac puts a bullet in her.'

The man grunted. 'And another bullet in young Jamie.'

Bella didn't know what to do. She was trapped. Terror seeped through her like ice. She felt sick at the thought of how she'd been fooled by Jamie Stoddard. He wasn't the kind, affectionate young man she'd supposed. Mark was right. Jamie had used her. By trapping her, he'd put her life in danger.

She was about to hand over the money when she caught sight of something in the corner of her eye. A patch of blue uniform appeared briefly behind the two interlopers. Bella wasn't completely alone. Mark had raised the alarm.

Sister Judd tried to sound calm .

'Give them what they want, Nurse Denton,' she suggested. 'It's the only way.'

'She can't – it's mine,' insisted Jamie.

The heavy man took a step towards Bella

and held out his hand.

'Last chance, sweetheart. Give it here – or else!'

'All right,' she said. 'You can have it.'

But she didn't just pass it to him. Flicking the elastic bands from the wads of notes, she flung them in his face so he was caught off balance for a moment, in a snowstorm of money. The security guards seized their moment. Two of them tackled him and a third grabbed the woman from behind.

There was a sharp *crack* as the gun went off in the struggle, but the bullet lodged harmlessly in the ceiling. More security men rushed in to help overpower them. The man was eventually dragged off and, screaming with rage, the woman was taken out after him.

Mark appeared in the doorway.

'Bella! Are you all right?' he cried.

'Yes, fine,' she said.

And then she fainted.

Gordy crept furtively down the back lane until he reached the garden wall. He shinned up it and dropped into the back garden of the house. As he let himself in, he heard Karlene's voice in the living room.

'That sounds like him now, Jessica!' she said.

Gordy's heart missed a beat but raucous laughter told him his friends were playing a trick on him. The dreaded Jessica was not in the house. Mark, Karlene and Suzie were lounging in chairs, each with a cup of coffee.

Gordy flopped down on the sofa, relieved. 'Very funny, Kar!' he said.

'How long are you going to go on climbing over the garden wall to get in here?' she asked.

'Just until the coast is clear,' he said, wearily.

'I thought you'd told Jessica to cool it – that things were finished between you.'

'I did but she's difficult to shake off. Kish offered me his brother as a bodyguard.'

'There's another form of protection,' said Suzie.

'A suit of armour?'

'No, Gordy. A girlfriend. If Jessica sees you out with someone else, she'll soon get the message.'

'I doubt it,' he said, gloomily. 'Jessica's the

persistent type. I'll have to lie low for a bit longer. That girl is ruining my life.'

'Don't exaggerate, Gordy,' said Karlene. 'It's only a temporary problem. Think of some of the patients at the hospital. They've *really* got things to worry about. Daisy, for instance – she's going to be permanently disabled.'

'Is that the girl who lost her leg?' asked Mark. 'I thought she was making good progress now.'

'She's talking to her mother again, if that's what you mean. That was a real triumph for me and Tony. But it will take time before she and her mum are friends again. But at least Daisy doesn't blame her for the accident any more.'

'Is she coming to terms with her accident now?' asked Suzie.

'Slowly, yes – but it will be a long haul.'

'I wish someone would amputate Jessica from my life,' moaned Gordy. 'I'd soon come to terms with that.'

Bella came downstairs and joined her friends in the living room. She was wearing a tight pink dress and a pair of long silver earrings.

'You look fantastic!' said Mark.

'Thanks. I bought this dress to cheer myself up after all the hassle of the last few days.' Bella sighed. 'I'll miss out on that trip to Paris, but I'm glad I discovered what a rat Jamie Stoddard really is.'

'Mark did warn you,' reminded Karlene.

'Next time I'll listen to him,' she promised.

'I still don't understand exactly what happened,' said Gordy. 'Can someone explain it in words of one syllable?'

'Yes,' said Bella. 'Jamie conned me. He told me he was an investment banker. What that really meant was he invested time in robbing banks. He got lucky last time round, he netted half a million pounds.'

'So why did his mates try to kill him?'

'He double-crossed them,' she said. 'He wanted to keep all the cash for himself. He was working with Loomis.'

'Who's that?'

'The driver on the bank job. Loomis was the man who turned up at the hospital in the dark glasses. That big thug, Mac, had beaten the truth out of him. Loomis wanted out. He turned up at the hospital and threw his share of the takings back at Jamie. Twenty thousand pounds of it.'

'That was what was in the package he gave Bella,' said Mark.

Gordy was still baffled. 'But what about his sister?'

'She wasn't Jamie's sister,' snorted Bella. 'She and Mac were his accomplices until he did the dirty on them. When they failed to blow him up, they tried to get their money out of him. That's why they came after me. That woman forced

Jamie to admit he'd given the package to me.'

'But that only contained twenty thousand quid,' noted Gordy. 'It doesn't seem much of a haul for two of them.'

'There was something else in that package,' said Mark.

'Yes,' added Bella. 'A safe-deposit key. Jamie had the rest of the cash hidden away. That key was on a chain round his neck most of the time. He decided it would be safer in the Bella Denton bank vault.'

Mark grinned. 'The suitcase under her bed.'

'You were a real heroine in Mendip Ward,' said Karlene, 'when you helped to catch those villains.'

'It's all part of the service,' said Bella, airily.

'Who's taking you out tonight?'

'Damian.'

'I thought you'd dumped him,' said Gordy.

'Well, Damian thought the hospital had dumped him as well,' added Suzie with a wry smile. 'He'd been charged with negligence and the chairman of the Board of Inquiry sent for him. Damian was convinced he'd be told to leave the hospital.'

'And was he?' asked Mark.

'No. That was another con – Mr Mullins, the boy's father, was trying to screw money out of the hospital by threatening to sue them. He claimed that Damian treated his son for a head injury but missed the boy's rib damage. When they x-rayed the boy the next day, he really did have cracked ribs.'

'How did Damian miss that in his examination?'

'He didn't, Mark.'

'No,' said Suzie. 'What happened was this. The first accident on the bike left the boy with concussion and he had a night in hospital. The next day, would you believe, he gets back on his bike and collides with a lamppost. Result?'

'Cracked ribs.'

'Yes, Mark. Mr Mullins saw his chance. He rushed his son back to Casualty for an x-ray, saying that the rib injuries had been caused by the *first* accident. Luckily, they realized what he was up to so Damian's in the clear. Mr Mullins made him the target for his crafty scheme.'

'Then I sympathise with him,' said Bella. 'I was a target as well. It's no fun, I can tell you.'

'What about me?' wailed Gordy. 'I'm Jessica's target. She wants to score a bull's-eye every time!'

'I suppose Mrs Collier was a target, too,' added Karlene. 'A target for Daisy's anger. I really hope they can work things out between them. They need each other.'

Bella looked in the mirror and flicked her hair back. Gordy smelt her perfume.

'You've put your best scent on for him, Bel. What made you decide to go out with Damian again?'

'I was really mean to him. He deserves another chance.' She grinned.

The doorbell rang and Bella glanced through the window to see Damian waiting outside. She couldn't resist a joke.

'Gordy! It's Jessica! Shall I let her in?'

'NO-O-O-O!' he yelled.

And dived over the sofa to hide behind it.

Now Gordy was the target – for their laughter.

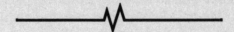

CITY HOSPITAL SERIES
by Keith Miles

Discover City Hospital and the five young recruits who work there. Experience the high drama and the humour of life in a large, modern hospital. Everything from romance to radiotherapy, drama to drudgery, fun to fatigue. If you can take the pressure, it's all here!

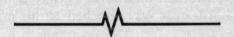

CITY
HOSPITAL

NEW BLOOD

As soon as the ambulance stopped, its doors opened and the stretcher was lifted swiftly but gently to the ground. The small boy with the chubby face lay pale and motionless on his back. As one of the paramedics wheeled him into Casualty, another walked alongside, holding the plastic bottle that was attached to his arm by a tube.

Dr Damian Holt was waiting with a nurse in a bay that was curtained off by a plastic sheet. One look at the patient told him that the boy was in a critical condition.

Two lives hang in the balance at City Hospital - but Suzie's involvement in the first means her life is in danger too

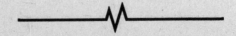

CITY HOSPITAL

FEVER

Bella was stunned. 'Mrs Elliott isn't *dead* is she?'

'Yes, I'm afraid so. We did all we could but...' Her voice trailed off – she looked shocked and confused herself.

'What was the cause of death?'

Sister Morgan's face changed. Bella had never seen her look like that before; a look of fear and bewilderment. It was as if she'd come up against something completely outside her experience. It scared her. She bit her lip and shook her head sadly.

'We don't know, Bella,' she admitted. 'We just don't know.'

Feelings run to fever-pitch at City Hospital – will someone crack under the strain?

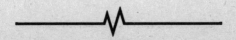

CITY
HOSPITAL

EMERGENCY

Out!' repeated Jez. 'Or she gets it!'

Two more security guards had arrived and were looking in through the window. They watched as their colleague slowly backed out of the office with the two male nurses. Jez Halliday held the advantage for the moment and there was little that they could do. Sister Poole and Bella Denton were hostages.

'Stay back!' he yelled. 'Or I blow her brains out.

A high-tension hostage situation puts the whole of City Hospital on edge – who will break the deadlock?

FLAMES

Karlene retched as the smoke got into her throat. Coughing himself, Mark led her away from the blaze. For a few minutes, they could do nothing but wait and watch. After what seemed like a lifetime to the waiting crowd, the inferno seemed finally under control. There was a loud hissing noise and two firemen with breathing apparatus were checking to see if it was safe to go into the building.

A new sound cut through the pandemonium. It was the high-pitched scream of a girl, who was racing along the street towards them.

'No!' she shrieked. 'Not *our* house!'

Emotional trauma is part of daily life in City Hospita - but can the new recruits cope with personal crises too?

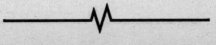

CITY
HOSPITAL

COMA

Suzie was holding Charlotte's hand and stroking it. Music was still playing in the background. Half the contents of Charlotte's bedroom were now around her. It was then that the miracle happened.

Charlotte's lips moved. At first, Suzie didn't believe what she'd seen. Had she been mistaken? Or was it just a nervous spasm? Keeping up the flow of talk, she watched carefully. It happened again. Her lips moved slightly and Suzie heard a low moaning sound. Charlotte was trying to speak.

Tension in City Hospital keeps the new recruits on call – physically and emotionally...